CW00833478

36 HOURS

B J WOSTER

36 Hours
B.J. Woster

ISBN: 9781957496184

© 2022 Literary Adventures
All Rights Reserved
All rights reserved. No part of this publication may be reproduced, stored in a retrieval system, or transmitted in any form or by any means, electronic, mechanical, photocopying, recording, or otherwise, without the prior permission of the publishers. Any person who commits any unauthorized act in relation to this publication may be liable to criminal prosecution and civil claims for damages.

ALSO BY B J WOSTER

Parenting in the 21 Century: A horror story

Juvenile Stories (ages 6-12)

Ehtaria: a land of their own

I Am Proud of Who I Am (15-book series)

For more information: www.barbarawosterauthor.com

For my family, without whose love and support this book would never have been written. I love you all dearly.

CHAPTER 1

October 30, 6:30 p.m.

B rooke Madison watched the numbers on the LED display descend slowly—eight, seven, six—moving closer toward her destination in the lower level of the parking garage. Four, three, two...the closer the elevator got, the more nervous she became. Sweat popped out along her upper lip; her body reacting to the nervous tension, firing throughout every nerve ending. She felt ashamed that she couldn't control the physical reaction.

The beep sounded, signaling her arrival, and it made her jump. She blinked and refocused on the LED display. *B-3*, it showed. Her level. She blinked again, drawing in deep shaky breaths, as the doors parted with a gentle whoosh; but she didn't move. As usual, she couldn't move. Paralytic fear set in, and her shame intensified, for she knew she *would* move—eventually.

She felt absurd and mentally berated herself.

You're behaving like a dog on the Fourth of July, afraid of the fireworks—quivering and shivering, hiding. You should be more than able to come and go from a parking garage elevator without having a near heart attack. Get a grip girl! You are strong and capable, so start acting like it!

She *should* be more than ready to move on—to move out of the elevator without her knees knocking loudly; without her heart pounding as if trying to flee her chest; without her lungs fighting for every breath. She shouldn't be worried that there was a bogeyman lurking in the shadows; but she was.

The doors began to slide closed, and she instinctively reached out to punch the *open-door* button. The door quietly obeyed the command and Brooke took a determined step toward the portal, glancing about in a manner that was borderline paranoid. If anyone observed her behavior, she could care less if they snickered because she felt justified in her abnormal fear of parking garages.

Justified because of Sandra McIntyre.

She'd always been a bit nervous over the dark, dank, enclosed levels of parking structures. It was a nervousness bordering on phobia, but she managed to curb it by moving to and from her vehicle at a rapid clip. She chose to continue parking on these levels instead of the open airy levels above because she was determined to conquer her fear.

But that was before Sandra McIntyre. Now she doubted she'd ever feel able to conquer this fear. It was the thought of tomorrow, parking on the upper level, which gave her the strength she needed to break her paralysis.

She took another deep breath and stepped tentatively just outside of the elevator, her hands slightly behind her, ready to stop the doors should she find herself unable to continue. Of course, she *would* continue; knew she had to if she was to get to her car and leave this place; a place that no longer represented a mere structure for automobiles, rather invoked an irrational dread and uncertainty. Still, she shouldn't have to stand at the ready: ready to prevent the elevator doors slipping closed, ready to leap back into the safety offered by that chilly metal box—but she did, all because of Sandra McIntyre.

She just wished her mind would stop inventing illusions of horror. She knew that she had only herself to blame for the paranoia that now gripped her, and her shame turned to anger. She took a tentative step forward, cringing as she finally permitted the doors to slide closed behind her.

Perhaps, she thought, the garage would seem less daunting if the lights were all in working order. She was certain that the owner would be eager to replace the bulbs, after what happened to Sandra. She glanced up at the ceiling and counted the number of non-functioning or empty sockets between the elevator and the space where she knew her car to be: twelve, by her count; twelve out of thirty. That was far too many in her estimation. The dimness leant a sinister air to the cool, pervasive dampness of the garage.

With a deep breath, she took another step away from the elevator, moving toward her parking slot, her stilettos clicking off each rapidly increasing step across the oil-stained concrete flooring.

Breathe and just remember what to do if you are attacked, she said tacitly, mentally reviewing everything she'd learned in her self-defense classes; classes she'd started taking on the recommendation of Sandra McIntyre.

She stumbled, and her hand shot toward a nearby beam to prevent falling.

"Fat lot of good those classes had done her..." She started cursing aloud, but then stopped. "No! I can't think like that. I can't believe that I am defenseless. The classes didn't fail Sandra; she simply hadn't been alert.

That's it. She simply hadn't paid attention to her surroundings. 'Always know what's happening around you' had been the instructor's first dictate. Well, I haven't yet made that mistake. I'm as alert as anyone can get."

She was so alert in fact that every nerve in her body jumped at every single noise, which caused it to tingle in a most uncomfortable fashion; much like the painful tingling feeling when a sleeping foot begins to waken.

She spotted her red Ford Mustang sitting nestled between a gray BMW and a burgundy Hummer. Her breathing eased a bit the closer she got until she was fairly laughing with relief when she reached the front of the car. She sighed deeply. If she didn't bring her insane irrationality back down to her customary, rational anxiety soon, she'd go completely bonkers.

"I may have to seek out a therapist, because my fear is getting out of hand," she conversed with herself, as she plopped her purse atop the hood and began rooting about in the large interior for her keys. This habit she hadn't yet changed as the self-defense instructor suggested.

"One of the biggest mistakes people make," he intoned during class, "is that people assume they will be able to get into their cars quickly; that they will be able to get to their keys and the safety of the car's interior before an assailant can attack."

Although she had made a mental decision to heed the instructor's warning, she had yet to latch her keys to her purse's exterior as he'd suggested; hadn't even purchased a carabiner yet. Now, with a sigh of frustration, she yanked the purse open wider, glaring inside, daring her keys to continue hiding beneath her wallet, umbrella, and other sundries.

"I think it's time to clean this out," she muttered, as she resorted to pulling out items one at a time, "and it's also time to downsize this monstrosity."

"Trick or treat," a voice whispered near her ear, and she jerked violently, knocking her purse to the ground, scattering the contents across the oily gray surface.

Her hands flailing, she spun and quickly struck a martial art pose: stance wide to provide balance, and her fists raised and ready to strike. The sight was so comical that the man who'd startled her chuckled. That pissed Brooke off, and she swung a fist and hit him hard in the upper arm and then swung the other fist and hit his shoulder. He backed away, but otherwise showed no outward sign of offense.

"*That* wasn't very nice," she snapped, bending to start picking up her belongings.

"At least you found your keys," Christian laughed, rubbing his upper arm. "You hit like a girl."

"Oh, that's not something we girls hear every day,"

Brooke snapped sarcastically. "What are you doing going around scaring people like that, anyway?" She asked in a tone that spewed fear and hostility. "And for your information, Halloween isn't until tomorrow."

When she realized that he hadn't stooped to assist her, she glared up at him, "This was your fault you know, so you could do the decent thing and help me collect my stuff."

"That's okay; you seem to have everything covered." He leaned against a nearby column and crossed his arms, his eyebrow raised as if in annoyance over having to wait for her. "Besides, I like these trousers, and don't want to pay to have them cleaned again so soon."

"You're a real gentleman, aren't you? What are you doing here anyway?" Brooke asked, reaching beneath her car to retrieve a extravagantly expensive tube of lipstick, cursing under her breath at the man for causing her to destroy a perfectly good pair of pantyhose.

"I happened to be in the neighborhood, preparing for an experiment that I'm going to be conducting. Anyway, I need a volunteer to help with that experiment. I knew you worked in the Bank of America Plaza, so I thought I'd stop by to see if I couldn't talk you into lending a hand. Thought it might do you some good since you've missed quite a few classes of late."

"I haven't thought of whether to continue the classes,"

she said, sliding further beneath her vehicle. She grabbed her lipstick and hairbrush, and then scooted from beneath the car, "I'm just not certain they are doing me any good."

"You were ready to take me on," Christian encouraged. "Would you have been able to do that much a month ago?"

Brooke shook her head, but it wasn't in response to his query, rather regarding her decision to drop the classes, "I'm sorry, but I'm not certain those classes are what I need right now." She stopped short of reminding him how futile those classes had proven for Sandra. "I'm sure that there are others in the class that can assist in your experiment."

"Oh, I have already elicited assistance from Consuela, and I could really use one more person to make it work."

"What kind of experiment?" Brooke asked politely, while she finished packing up her purse. She still had no intention of helping, but that didn't mean she wasn't curious.

"The kind that will help save lives."

Brooke looked at her martial arts instructor with an arched brow, expecting him to fill in the blanks, but he just stood, as if that would be enough of an incentive for her to say yes.

"Well, as important as that sounds," she said finally,

"I'm afraid I already have commitments in place over the next few days with my sister and her children. It is coming up on Halloween after all. I hope you're able to find someone. I really need to be going now."

She pressed the button on her fob. The alarm on her car beeped off and the lock opened. Brooke reached for the door handle, but a sudden pressure against her nose and mouth startled her.

"Would 'you don't have a choice in the matter' help you change your mind?" Christian whispered against her ear, holding onto the cloth tighter and pulling her up against his body, as Brooke's struggles intensified.

"You really shouldn't have missed so many classes, my dear," he murmured, "or you may have known what to do in this particular circumstance."

The last coherent thought she had, as her assailant lowered her body to the cold concrete, was that her instinct had failed her, just as it had Sandra. Her eyes fluttered closed, as a lone tear broke free. She was going to die.

CHAPTER 2

7:20 p.m.

H ello, sleepy head."
The voice broke through into her fog-filled mind and Brooke struggled to open her eyes completely; and keep them opened. She shook her head to clear the cobwebs that had developed, but that did no more than create a vertigo sensation, so she lie her head still and waited. It took a few minutes, but eventually clarity started to return; but not comprehension.

"Are you awake now?" The voice uttered so near to her ear that it startled her into opening her eyes fully; not a hint of drowsiness remained. When she turned her head, the sight of her abductor sitting so near to her, startled her so that alarm bells began ringing throughout her body. She struggled to pull herself away from him, finally managing to slide to a half-seated position against the headboard.

"You?" She croaked after taking several saliva-filled gulps to moisten her exceedingly dry mouth. She fought to sit up straighter, as anger replaced fear. "What in hell do you think you're playing at?" She whispered hoarsely. "I said that I *wouldn't* participate in your little experiment, or did you have a temporary bout of hearing loss after you asked me?"

Her abductor smiled, "I told you that I needed a participant, and as I already determined that you would do, I wasn't going to comb the neighborhood for someone else."

"This isn't funny, Christian," Brooke snapped, slipping slowly from the bed. She tested her ability to stand, then bent over to pick up her stilettos and headed for the door. "And I haven't time for your stupid games, or your stupid experiments. I'm outta here!"

Christian stepped in her path, "Sorry, Brooke, but I'm afraid you're with me for the long-haul."

"I beg your ever-loving pardon? What in hell are you talking about—long-haul? Just how long is this blasted experiment of yours supposed to last, anyway?"

"Thirty-six hours," Christian said patiently. "Well,

thirty-six once the actual experiment begins. If you count..."

"Thirty-six hours!" Brooke screeched, interrupting Christian's patronizing explanation. "I sure as hell do *not* have thirty-six hours to devote to you. I told you that my sister is expecting me. Now let me by," she barked angrily. When he again blocked the exit, she backed up a step and hurled a shoe at his head.

"I told you that I needed an assistant," Christian said, dodging the spiked heel. "And I explained, rather pleasantly I thought, that you were going to be that assistant. Now, no more petulance if you please." He pulled a disposable cell phone from his pant pocket, and then glanced at his watch. Seven-twenty-seven p.m.

"Is this some sort of test? Is that it?" Brooke asked, her gaze narrowing in anger, her breath heaving.

"If it had been, you'd have failed miserably, or did you think that slapping an attacker on the arm would deter him? Did you think standing by while the chloroform did its work was acceptable?" Christian retorted.

"I didn't slap, I punched, and I *know* you, you asshole! You're my martial arts instructor!" Brooke screamed. "So, I hardly expected you to abduct me using chloroform or...at all!"

Christian sighed, "It's time."

"I said I'm not participating..."

"You are going to dial *911*," he continued, ignoring her outburst.

"I said I'm...what?"

"When they answer, you will have thirty seconds to tell them everything you can; anything that will aid the police in locating you."

"I get to dial *911*?" Brooke asked, incredulous, but the astonishment didn't last for long as anger welled like a typhoon. "You know what? Screw you! Keep your damned phone. I'm not helping you and that's that!"

Christian sighed again and tossed the phone in her direction. "Go!"

Brooke caught the phone instinctively, but simply stared at it in defiance. "I'm not..." she started, but when he pressed a button on his watch to begin the count-down, her survival instincts kicked in and she pressed the emergency button.

"911, what is your emergency?"

"Hello, operator? My name is Brooke Madison. I've been kidnapped by a man named Christian Price..."

"Miss?"

"Please, you have to listen, I don't have a lot of time," Brooke pleaded. "I said that I've been kidnapped, and I bloody well need help."

"Do you know where you're being held," The operator droned dispassionately.

"If I knew that, it would have been the first thing I told you! All I can tell is that I'm in what looks like a warehouse of some sort. There's a window way up high. The square kind that looks like it belongs in a basement, only the room is too big to be a basement... Hey! Give me that back!"

"Hello, operator, this is Miss Madison's abductor," Christian relayed, putting a hand up to ward off Brooke's attempts to retrieve the phone. Her yelling, however, was making it difficult to talk to the operator, so he paused his conversation with a polite, "excuse me" and laid the phone on the floor.

He approached Brooke menacingly, which had her backing away, "Either hush now," he said in a calm that belied his anger at her, "or I may not give you thirty-six hours for this experiment. I'll end it now, and as ending it now would mean killing you, I don't think you want that."

Brooke stared at Christian wide-eyed, but his threat worked at silencing her tirade. He returned and picked up his phone. The *911* operator was trying to get his attention.

Hello, are you still there?

"I've returned, and I need you to listen to me well. This is not a joke. Please relay the following information to the police. Inform them that they have thirty-six hours to locate Brooke Madison, or she dies..."

"*Sir?*"

"I do hope you were paying attention because I won't be repeating what I just said. Your time starts—now!" Christian touched the button that effectively ended the call and then tucked the phone back into his pants pocket.

Brooke stared at him, wide-eyed, "Die?" She whispered. "You're going to kill me? You didn't say that this experiment was life or death. You said your experiments were to help save lives."

"I truly hope it doesn't end in death, Brooke," he said in such a truthful, sincere tone that Brooke felt tears well in her eyes. "I put my experiments in place to help save as many lives as is possible, but sometimes, to accomplish that, a few lives must be sacrificed. Again, I do hope that yours isn't one of them."

"Just tell me why?" She whispered, pleading. "Why? Why did you have to choose me for this? Surely there are plenty of other people you could have picked on," She screamed when he ignored her question and turned to leave.

"This will be over in thirty-six hours," he said softly. "All the police have to do is their job."

"Thirty-six hours and you'll let me go?" Brooke tried again.

"If the police come for you, you go free," he said. "If not…well then, the experiment is over."

"You're experimenting with my life, you bastard! You can't do this to me!" Brooke yelled, running at him like a football tight end. She collided with him, but he was ready for her and shoved her backward as she neared. She fell on her bottom and let out a squeal of humiliated anger.

"Actually, I already am doing this to you," he said, the flat tone of his voice belying the sadness in his gaze. "So, accept it and just sit peacefully and await the arrival of the police. That's all you have to do."

"But, why? What have I ever done to you? Are you just mad because I didn't want to help you? Is that it? Or because I failed your little test? Or was I a bad martial arts student and this is payback for not putting my keys on the outside of my purse?" Brooke cried, trying to stall his departure. "Wait! Please? Just…are you the one who killed Sandra?"

He turned and opened the door, stepping into the corridor before turning back to answer her question.

"You've done nothing to me, Brooke, and neither did Sandra," he replied softly, "but I'll say it again—someone has to be sacrificed if it means saving hundreds of others." He raised his hands to prevent any further questions. "No more histrionics now. I have to go, but before I do I want to thank you."

"What for—being an unwilling participant in your sadistic game?" Brooked snarled.

"No, I want to thank you for starting the police off on the wrong foot. It will be a good test to determine just what caliber of officer we have in this city."

"I don't know what you're talking..."

"My name isn't Christian Price."

CHAPTER 3

9:30 p.m.

The tape ended and Captain Gary Parsons, a tall, rugged, bald African American with a booming voice, turned to face two of his best detectives. "What do you make of it?" He asked, trying to maintain his calm, but his voice still reverberated around his too-compact office.

"He's a sick son-of-a-bitch." Theodore Wilson rubbed his hand along the back of his neck, hoping to rub free the tension building in his muscles. As his fingers ran along his neck, his mind drifted off momentarily that he'd forgotten to get his blonde locks cut. If he didn't do it soon, he'd start looking like a pop singer, rather than a detective. After a minute, he forced his thoughts back to the case, "What kind of twisted mind lets the victim call *911* and then informs her that he's going to kill her in thirty-six hours..."

"Thirty-four hours now," Detective Steven Hardwick interjected abstractly. Hardwick, a thirty-year veteran of the APD, glanced at his watch, his gaze falling on the tiny gray hairs surrounding the gold band. His thoughts flittered to all the gray hairs he viewed in the mirror at night, when his freshly washed black hair sprung awry in a mass of waves atop his head, a testament to his Italian heritage. Every morning, he slicked that hair down, not only to try to keep it regulation, but also to try to hide the gray hairs which revealed his age.

"Yeah, thirty-four hours," Wilson said, casting his partner a 'you're a wise ass' look.

"So, then, any more useful tidbits either of you want to add before I unleash you two on this guy?" The captain wanted this case off his desk and cleared quickly. Murderers were bad enough without them calling and taunting the police before committing the murder.

"His name isn't Christian Price," Hardwick said thoughtfully.

"Why would she..." Wilson started.

"She *knows* him as Christian Price, or he let his name

slip so she'd give the police a false start right out of the chute," the captain concluded.

"Which is both beneficial and not," Hardwick said. "Since we only have thirty-four hours..."

"Thirty-three and fifty-four minutes," Wilson interrupted, sardonically.

Hardwick looked at his watch, "Right," he said, cocking an eyebrow at Wilson. "There's something else. It could be nothing, but I think there's a connection to an open case."

"What case?" The captain asked. His brow arched. He hadn't heard of another case like this one.

"A few days ago, a body was found because of an anonymous tip. Sandra McIntyre. I still have the file on my desk."

"I know the case, but it's still under investigation," the captain interjected, "but I don't see the similarities. What made you think of it?"

"In reality it has a remarkably similar M.O...thirty-six hours." Hardwick sat back in his chair and mentally reviewed the file in his head that was currently in his inbox. "Sandra was reported missing by her husband at 8 a.m., October 26th. He said that a man had called him and told him that she'd been abducted. At precisely 8 p.m. on the 27th, thirty-six hours later, we get an anonymous tip that a body was discovered in the warehouse district. I'm still searching for evidence in that case."

"Just because Sandra McIntyre was found thirty-six hours after being reported missing, doesn't necessarily connect these cases," the captain interjected. "After all, there are glaring dissimilarities. First, the husband called *911* to report his wife missing; the victim didn't make the call. Second, an anonymous tip thirty-six hours later doesn't mean there was a deadline in place after which McIntyre was killed. It could have been anyone roaming the warehouse district..."

"The woman in this case stated that she was being held in a building that could possibly be a warehouse," Wilson piped up.

"Precisely," Hardwick concurred, "and approximately three days after Sandra McIntyre was found, Brooke Madison is abducted; and her abductor has given us thirty-six hours in which to locate her; and is, apparently, holding her captive in what could be a warehouse, yes. I think it's the same perpetrator; that he is simply changing his method of notification to the police to accomplish his goal within a set time period. Too many similarities, for me. I say we're dealing with the same killer."

"It could be a coincidence, but knowing how you feel about coincidences, I'm just going to let you explain the glaring dissimilarity, which would be..." the captain started, but paused long enough to allow Hardwick to respond.

"The *911* call. I didn't overlook it. I think that perhaps the perp has simply added a different twist to his M.O. Maybe to him the game wasn't stimulating enough last time. Maybe he feels the need to taunt the police, to get a rise in adrenaline. Maybe Brooke Madison doesn't have a husband for the kidnapper to call. Maybe having the spouse call didn't elicit enough attention as having the victim call. Any number of reasons, but I still think it's the same guy."

"Well, if they are connected somehow, then catching this guy is the highest priority. If he's upping the ante with each kill, it's going to get a whole lot messier. And if he intends to kidnap someone weekly, we'll have the makings of a serial killer pretty damned fast."

"I agree," Hardwick nodded. "At the same time, it's given us quite the jump in potentially solving the McIntyre murder also. In order to see this done, though, we're going to need extra manpower on this one, Captain. We're not only investigating an older case, but also trying to prevent a death from occurring in this new case—and thirty-six hours is a tight deadline."

The captain nodded, "Understood. Let's get Harding and Cortez in on this one." He nodded at Wilson, who got up from his chair to summon two of the other detectives sitting idle at their desks.

"Cortez, Harding, Captain wants y'all."

Emanuel Cortez looked up from his paperwork, "*Uno momento*," he called, brushing a loose curl from his face. He closed the file he'd been working on and placed it in the stack of files on the side of his desk, then stood and made his way over to where Antoine Harding sat, deep in conversation with someone on the phone.

Cortez smacked Harding on the arm, "Hey, *jefe*, the captain summoned. Get your black ass off the phone."

Antoine Harding sent Cortez an evil glare, then concluded his conversation, "Gotta go, baby. Duty, and all that shit. I'll speak at you later." He hung up the receiver and then stood, nearly bumping into Cortez, who was still hovering, "Wanna hold my hand, Cortez? Make sure I can find the captain's office? I can't see why you're invading my space otherwise."

"I can see why someone as ugly as you would go after a fine-looking Spaniard like myself..."

"Bullshit! Just get your ass in gear before the captain decides to bust both our butts for keeping him waiting."

The two detectives weaved their way through the bullpen, their continued banter drawing the gazes of their fellow detectives, who just shook their heads or rolled their eyes as they passed by. It wasn't until they reached the captain's office that they ceased their idiocy and placed on their professional faces.

"Captain?" Cortez greeted, nodding to Hardwick and Wilson. "What gives?"

"We've got a situation," the captain said. "Another woman's been kidnapped. We think it's connected to the murder that took place a few days ago, since the perpetrator has given us only thirty-six hours to find her."

"Now, thirty-three..."

"Drop it, Wilson!" The captain snapped, "If you can't add anything constructive here, then shut the hell up! Cortez, Harding, you two will back up Hardwick and Wilson on this one. He'll fill you in."

"Captain, just because this kidnapping, and McIntyre's, fell within our zone, doesn't mean that he's holding her here. We may need the cooperation of the other districts," Harding stated. "We know that Atlanta's a big city with different zones, but a killer might not think that way; wouldn't necessarily think to keep his kills localized to one district."

"True," the captain concurred. "I'll get in touch with the other zone commanders. See what they can do to assist, but you know that departmental cooperation isn't a given. The other districts have their own loonies to deal with."

"I know, but most loonies don't challenge the police

so directly. Most times they're just dealing with gang bangers trying to do away with their rivals," Cortez replied, his tone sharp.

"Not very fair of you, Cortez," the captain chastised lightly. "You know that, even though a majority of crime in most of our districts are gang related, we still have the odd homicide to contend with—like now."

"Yeah, but two of those that just happened to get dumped in our lap from a potential serial killer, so any help given wouldn't go without a huge thank you and a keg of beer," Wilson added.

The captain sighed, "I'll see what miracle I can pull out of my ass. You four see about catching this guy and saving the girl."

All four detectives filed out of the captain's office. The captain watched them go and leaned back in his chair with a heavy sigh. Sometimes he hated this job.

"What are we looking at?" Harding asked as they approached Hardwick's desk.

"As I said in the captain's office, I think there might be a connection with our two recent victims. Same guy. Definitely a similar M.O." Hardwick handed over the McIntyre file and continued as Harding and Cortez scanned the contents. "I'm basing it on two small details: the thirty-six-hour window and the *911* call, even though one was placed by the spouse and the other by the victim."

"What about the warehouse connection?" Wilson asked.

"Places are too fluid. If he plans to continue killing, he could easily switch his kill sites if police presence in the warehouse districts increases, so while we have one death in the warehouse district, and potentially a hold site there also, let's not dwell on that too much right now, except as a possible for a search grid. Anyway, if we do have the start of a serial killer on our hands..." The phone rang, interrupting his explanation. "Hardwick," he answered, frustrated at having his thoughts disturbed. He pointed to a couple of chairs, then settled in his own chair. The three men rolled over their chairs and pulled them in a semi-circle around Hardwick's desk.

Front desk, sir. I have a message for you and a call.

"Message?" Hardwick pulled over a notepad and snatched a pen from an old coffee cup.

Message from Officer Patterson, the front desk droned. *He's at the scene of the kidnapping. Found her purse and car at her office's parking garage.*

"Get in touch with Officer Patterson and tell him that I'll be out there shortly. Have the location ready when I stop by on my way out."

Will do.

"Other message?"

Line three.

"The caller's holding?" Hardwick glanced down at the flashing light on his phone.

Yes, sir.

"Take a message," Hardwick snapped, impatient to begin work on the investigation. He hung up the receiver. "So, as I was saying, if we do have the start of a serial killing spree..." The phone rang again. "Damn!" He snatched up the receiver again, "Sergeant, just hold all of my calls and messages, until I'm headed out, okay? I'm rather preoccupied right now."

It's line three, sir.

"I said to take a message, Sergeant."

I tried, sir, but he insists on speaking to the man who's been put in charge of the kidnapping...

That's as far as the front desk officer got before Hardwick disconnected again. He punched the blinking white lit up *3*, followed by the speaker button.

"Detective Hardwick."

Detective Hardwick, the voice said, *this is Christian Price.*

All four men pulled notepads and pens to begin jotting notes, thoughts, anything that might help them get the most out of this phone call.

"What can I do for you, Mr. Price?" Hardwick asked.

I wanted to let you know that I don't want any harm to come to Brooke Madison...

"If you can lie about your name, why should I believe you about this?" Hardwick asked. Eyebrows raised around the desk at the belligerent tone.

Ah! That's good, Detective. You've already determined that I'm using an alias. Perhaps there is hope this time so that I won't have to move beyond Brooke.

"This time?" Hardwick asked. "Are you referring to Sandra McIntyre; and what do you mean "move beyond Brooke"?"

My my, you've connected Sandra to me. It's nice to speak to a detective, finally, with a brain to go with any sort of brawn he might have. I'm well pleased, I must say. Perhaps Brooke does stand a chance with you on the case. If only you'd been there in the past.

"It would have been nice, yes. Had you allowed Sandra the same courtesy of calling *911...*"

I wasn't referring to Sandra, but there's nothing that can change the past, so it's best to focus our attentions on Brooke, the caller interrupted, a genuine sadness in his tone. *I truly don't want to kill her; didn't want to kill any of them, you know. I just want the police to do their jobs.*

"Someone get on that," Hardwick whispered, covering the mouthpiece. Cortez leapt from his chair, ran back to his desk, and began punching at his keyboard. "What others are you talking about?" He asked the man known as Price.

I said that wasn't important. Only Brooke is important. Focus only on finding her, he replied. *I only called to encourage you to do your best. I truly don't want any harm...*

"Then let her go," Hardwick pressed.

I can't do that.

"So, if we can't find her, you're going to murder her?"

I wouldn't call it murder, Price countered.

"Taking another's life is murder in my book," Hardwick said, and Wilson arched an eyebrow again in his direction.

"Should you be antagonizing him like this," he whispered, leaning close to Hardwick's ear.

Hardwick shook his head and pressed a finger to his lips, and Wilson sat back with a frustrated sigh. In his estimation, if Hardwick persisted, he may provoke the man into upping his timetable.

Think of me as a lab technician, or, better yet, a scientist, Price was saying.

"A scientist?" Hardwick asked.

Yes. When scientists inject experimental drugs into the tiny, helpless body of a mouse and that mouse dies—is the scientist put on trial for murder, or is it considered justifiable homicide; the taking of one life to preserve hundreds or even thousands of others?

"There's considerable difference between a mouse and a human being," Hardwick retorted, shaking his head in disbelief at the man's insane justifications. "You sound too intelligent than to believe that hogwash." Hardwick could almost see the smile on the other man's face when he responded.

True, I don't consider them on the same scale, Price said, *but what I'm doing is not much different. After all, if I need to take the life of one—or more—to save lives of many more, then to me it's worth the cost.*

"And who gave you permission to make those sorts of decisions?" Hardwick barked, and both Wilson and Harding winced.

My wife, came the whispered instantaneous reply.

"I see," Hardwick sighed as the man's motivation became glaringly apparent, which also gave the detective his first insight into who he was dealing with. Nothing was more dangerous than a killer with a moral agenda. "I'm truly sorry for your loss." Hardwick pointed a finger at Harding. He nodded and leapt to his feet, heading toward his own computer to start a search on crimes of women in their district.

I believe you are, Price said softly. *Find her, Detective. Please don't make me kill her.*

"Then provide us a clue or give us more time. We

can't begin an effective investigation at this hour of the night."

I wish I could, Price said, and his voice held a genuinely sympathetic tone, *but if I do, then what will have been gained?*

"The life of a woman," Hardwick answered.

No, Detective, Price said, his tone shifting rapidly from sympathy to anger, *the continuing incompetence of the local police. I don't wish to harm Miss Madison, Detective, but make no mistake, I will do so—without reservation.*

"I'm sorry to hear that," Hardwick said, "but you should know that my fellow officers and I will do everything within our power to stop you."

That's what I'm counting on, Price said sharply. *Find her and my experiments will cease here in Atlanta. If you don't, she dies, and we'll start all over again. Don't doubt me when I say my experiments will continue until you guys get it right.*

The line went dead. Hardwick plopped back in his chair and tossed his pencil on his desk, "That was interesting. I don't doubt, now, that we have a potential self-confessed serial killer here. He may have committed one murder here in Atlanta, but from all he said, I have a feeling he's left bodies strewn elsewhere. Shit!" He exclaimed suddenly.

"What's wrong?" Wilson asked.

"We failed to think to start a trace!" Hardwick snapped, shaking his head. He really wanted to hit something. He glanced at his watch. Thirty-four hours and thirty-five minutes. Time was ticking away fast, too fast. Most cases went cold in the first twenty-four hours, making that a critical window; however, if given enough time, many of those cold cases were solved because evidence came to the forefront that may have been hidden or overlooked prior.

Giving the police a mere thirty-six hours in which to prevent a homicide was thumbing a nose at critical investigatory steps. In fact, forcing officers to spend a straight thirty-six hours on an investigation could ultimately prove detrimental. Sleep deprivation leant its way to mistakes and oversights. He wished he could send his detectives home for the night to get some rest and return bright and early, since there wasn't much any of them could do at this late hour; but he knew that wouldn't be prudent. There was still investigating to do and warehouses to search. He only hoped he and his fellow officers could prevent making mistakes that would lead to the death of another woman in his jurisdiction. He glanced at the clock—thirty-four hours, thirty-two minutes.

Hardwick stood and made his way over to Cortez and Harding.

"Nothing can be done about that now. We'll just need

to remember to trace the call should he call again. Wilson and I are going to head on over to the crime scene. See what's been discovered if anything. Cortez, narrow your search for any similar M.O. Focus on crimes where the perpetrator held the victim for thirty-six hours or had the victim dial *911*. Entire east coast database, not just Atlanta."

"I'm on it," Cortez said, turning back to face his screen.

"Harding, I want you to conduct a search also, but I want you to narrow your parameters to homicides, solved or unsolved, of women, thirty to fifty..."

"Why so restricted?" Wilson interrupted. "I mean, what if this guy's wife was twenty-six when she was killed?"

"It's a chance we have to take," Hardwick said.

"Besides, we haven't time to cover a full age spectrum," Harding added. "There's simply too many murders, especially women."

"But, again, why that age range?" Wilson pressed.

"Listening to his voice, how old would you guess he is?" Hardwick asked.

"Obviously, I couldn't say with any certainty, but if I had to hazard a guess—late forties, early fifties."

"Why?"

"I don't understand?"

"Why not twenty or seventy?"

"Um," Wilson started, pursing his lips in thought.

"He's calm and articulate. There's a maturity to his voice," Hardwick said, jumping in with his explanation. He had neither the time nor inclination to re-train a detective in identification indicators or profiling. "His grieving has passed, and now he's trying to fix what he conceives is broken, so that no one else gets hurt."

"And a twenty-year-old..."

"Angrier," Hardwick interjected with a sigh. "A twenty-year-old who suffers this type of loss is often angry, violent, and vindictive. A much older man would see anything that happens as having lived long enough and therefore is fate or part of life's end. A middle-aged man may accept the loss, but, as in this case, could attempt to set right perceived wrongs."

"Which is why he's been a detective far longer than any of us," Cortez said lightly of Hardwick.

"But what if the man lost his wife when he was in his twenties and he's just now getting around to retribution?" Wilson persisted, refusing to accept Hardwick's logic as sound. There simply were too many unsolved homicides to be overlooking them based on a hunch—even if it were a reasonable hunch.

"We'd have caught him by now," Hardwick said confidently, hoping to cease the barrage of questions. "Look, even if the case is ten or twenty years old, I'm pretty certain it's within the time frame."

"What's if it's older?" Wilson asked, unwilling to be deterred. He didn't like feeling stupid, and he certainly didn't like instructions on a search that made little-to-no sense to him.

"We haven't time to focus on what-ifs right now, or the time to run an expanded search," Hardwick responded with more than a hint of impatience. "Listen, if our investigation turns up nothing, we'll broaden the parameters."

When it appeared as if Wilson would continue to argue, he turned his back on him, turning to address Cortez. "Have dispatch contact us when you turn up anything of value; and don't forget, guys, we're racing against time on this one. We can't allow ourselves any lapses in mental acuity, so whatever you need to do to stay alert over the next thirty-four hours, do it! Once you've compiled your results and are confident that you can't do anything more, join your fellow officers in the field. There isn't much more we can do tonight than canvas warehouses in the district. It may be shooting at fish with a pellet gun, but we may get lucky and hit something."

CHAPTER 4

As soon as Christian had Brooke secured and got the APD fired up about finding her, he headed back to the apartment of another student in his martial arts class that he'd temporarily moved into. The one thing he always did, during his first two attempts at getting the police to perform their duty, was to prepare carefully so to prevent getting caught. Part of that preparation included: finding a base of operations, identifying the first two women he planned to use in his experiments—in this case Sandra and Brooke; and to find suitable locations where those experiments were to take place. It generally took him a week or two to get things underway, but once things got rolling, it went smoothly for him because there wasn't any flying by the seat of his pants.

It was only if the police failed in their attempts with victims one and two that things got derailed for him a bit, but he preferred not to worry over that eventuality until it happened; especially as he always hoped and prayed it wouldn't. In the other cities in which he'd conducted his experiments, he'd only had to abduct and set up a third experiment because those departments had failed in saving the first two women. Every time that happened it made him think he needed to start planning for at least three *assistants* to his experiments. Detective Hardwick, however, gave him hope that this department may just succeed where some of the others had failed—although they hadn't saved Sandra, which made him release a sigh of frustration.

He pulled into the apartment complex only a few blocks from the warehouse district in which Brooke was located and parked in the far recesses. After scanning the lot carefully to ensure there was not a lot of foot traffic, he got out of his vehicle and made his way to the third-floor apartment of Consuela Montenegro.

A quick peek in the bedroom showed her to be sleeping soundly. He stepped into the room and did his routine inspection of her IV drip and changed her Depends undergarment; then stepped into the bathroom and ran warm water into a bucket he kept next to the tub, along with a sponge, a towel, and a sheet of plastic. He tested the water, then collected all the supplies and headed back to the bedroom.

"Have to keep you clean during your long, induced sleep," he whispered conversationally, as he rolled her naked body aside to lay out the plastic. Once it was set, he rolled her back, then set about giving her a sponge bath. To anyone watching his gentle attentive behavior, Christian would appear an intense paradox, for he treated those with whom he stayed with a kind respect, which bespoke of his value for life; whereas he sadistically ended the lives of others whom he abducted for his experimentation phases.

When he was satisfied that she was clean, he took a towel and dried her thoroughly, the rolled her over again and dried her backside, then slipped on another pair of Depends. He carefully collected the plastic sheeting and placed it in the tub to dry. Once her needs were tended to, he covered her respectfully, then returned to the living room.

"Time to see if there's been any updates reported," he murmured, and turned on the news. Nothing new was on, just a rehash of the abduction, and more information about who Brooke was, so he turned the volume down and then checked the camera to see what Brooke was up to. He shook his head and grinned, "Right where I left you."

He glanced at his watch. It was getting late. He went to his satchel and pulled out a bottle of Valerian and Melatonin. If he were to stay on top of things tomorrow, he needed some rest tonight. He popped several pills and then went to lie down on the couch. Too bad the APD weren't going to be getting any rest tonight. At least he hoped they'd take this seriously and not spend their time wastefully.

CHAPTER 5

Brooke sat on the edge of the mattress and took in her surroundings. She didn't know what she was going to do but sit here and wait to die couldn't be her only option. She had to find a way out. Christian was certain that all she needed to do was wait patiently, and the local police would swoop in to save the day. Should she heed that advice? Had Sandra heeded that advice? If so, it hadn't done her much good.

Besides, patiently waiting wasn't her strongest character trait. She considered herself a woman of action. Her belief? If you want to accomplish anything, you can't sit on your butt and wait on others to do it for you. Of course, by that reasoning, she needed to do something other than sit on her own ass.

She let her gaze travel the room again, her focus narrowed on any form of escape route. The only apparent avenue of escape was either the door—bolted—or the window, which was far too high for her to reach.

"Argh," she exclaimed loudly, standing, and pacing the room. She smacked the wall in frustrated anger, and then shook her hand as the tingling vibration shot up her arm. "Damn it all to hell and back, there has to be a way out of here." She bent at the waist, placed her hands on her knees and drew in deep, relaxing breaths. When her nerves were calm again, she stood and spun in a slow circle, doing another sweep of the room, slowly taking in every detail. One of the things that registered was that the room really wasn't as large as it seemed, the expanse more illusory minus the absence of furnishings. The only things in the room were a bed, a toilet, and a refrigerator. As old as those items were, it was readily apparent that this place had been abandoned long ago, and obviously wasn't part of the overhaul being done on warehouses throughout the city...at least not currently. She scanned the room again and her gaze stopped on the refrigerator.

"Could that be a solution?" She murmured and then walked over to it, turned, and tried to gauge how far it was to the space beneath the window. It was on the other side of the room, which didn't seem that far, but visual distance was subjective because variables played a huge factor in whether she would be able to move it at all. Fifteen feet could easily feel like a hundred feet if conditions worked against her. The first thing that crossed her mind was weight. There was not only her weight to consider, but the weight of the fridge. It was an older, heavier model. Not constructed from lightweight fiberglass, like today's refrigerators. Friction was another factor for making the distance less reachable with ease. The floor was not a smooth glassy surface on which something might glide easily across; rather, it was a pitted and bumpy concrete floor that could cause all sorts of grief when trying to move a large, unwieldy item; and on closer examination, it appeared as if there were sections of oily residue as if this had housed automobiles at one point. That could prove slick and treacherous.

Still, she'd examined all other options, and this appeared her only one. She started by trying to psyche herself up, "Okay girl, you did not spend all of those evenings at the gym for nothing. You may be petite, but you are also strong and capable."

She drew in a deep, cleansing breath again and let it out with a whoosh, pulled her brunette hair up and looped it in a knot. She wished she had a hair tie, but knotting her hair was better than having it fall into her face continually while she worked. Next, she placed her hands on each side of the fridge. With a loud grunt, she gave a mighty pull.

It didn't move.

"Oh, no you don't!" She muttered angrily. "You happen to be the only thing available to reach my only avenue of escape, so you bloody well better move!"

She put her shoulder against the side of green, antiquated Kenmore and using every muscle from shoulder to toes, emitted a great grunt of effort. It tipped slightly, threatening to overturn. She sighed loudly and stepped back to reassess.

"Okay, brute strength isn't going to get the job done," she ruminated, abstractly swiping rusted flakes from her shirt; and then a memory of her childhood moved to the forefront of her mind; an image of her father moving their refrigerator. He didn't use brute strength, rather rocked the fridge back and forth.

"Okay, so then let's try that," she said to herself. She stretched her hands out and grasped each side, then pushed one side and then the other. It wasn't necessarily the easiest thing, but it was working. Slowly, inch-by-aggravatingly-slow-inch, the refrigerator wobbled, shook, but moved closer to the opposite wall.

CHAPTER 6

Hardwick and Wilson drove in silence most of the distance to the crime scene. Eventually though, Wilson, who'd been all but pouting the entire time, spoke up, "I don't appreciate you shooting me down back there."

"What are you talking about?"

"Back at headquarters. My concerns regarding your limited search parameters were justified and needed voicing."

"And voice those concerns you did; and explain why we didn't have time for anything more than I suggested, I did. I didn't shoot you down, Wilson, we simply do not have the time to satisfy every question bounding through your brain. So, get past it."

Wilson clenched his jaw and nodded tersely. "Fine, so why did you just drive by Bank of America Plaza? Isn't that where we were headed? Does that mean you don't think it's necessary that we head to the crime scene? Is it a waste of time to ask why?"

"Not a waste of time, no. We're not going to the crime scene, because it registered that it isn't likely to reveal anything that Patterson wouldn't let us know about; and any DNA evidence, which is unlikely to exist because of the conditions at the scene, won't be processed tonight either. That reminds me," Hardwick continued as he made a U-turn at the next intersection, "get on the com and have dispatch inform Patterson that we won't be meeting him at the crime scene. He was expecting us."

Wilson complied and then turned to address Hardwick, "Now what?" he asked.

Hardwick sighed, "Okay, Brooke Madison told the *911* operator that she was being held in what appeared to be a warehouse."

"Yeah, but most of Atlanta's warehouse districts have been revamped; modernized. Are there even any abandoned warehouses left standing where someone could hide a person away for thirty-six hours undetected?"

"This guy stashed McIntyre away somewhere for thirty-six hours; and there are kidnappers who manage to hide their victims away undetected in their own basements. Besides revamped doesn't mean inhabited. Many of the units are still vacant, making it a good hiding place, whether vacant or abandoned."

"You aren't building any confidence in our ability to find her, you know."

Hardwick sighed loudly, "Atlanta is a big city and since the warehouse description is the best link we have right now, then it's the lead we need to follow up on."

"Where do you want me to have the officers dispatched? Unless you think we alone can search all of the warehouses in and around Atlanta?"

"I don't think the whole of the APD Zone 5 has enough officers to cover all of the warehouses in Atlanta. Still, it's the only place we have to start, so have a couple of black and whites meet us at Castleberry Hill. Then dispatch additional units to the west side to check out the Design District."

"What about the Metropolitan District?"

"Yeah, may as well, and have a few police dispatched to the Diamond Street project. Then alert all other black and whites to investigate any abandoned building they may stumble upon during their routine patrols. No stone unturned. This guy may have killed before in other cities, and may have slipped one past us, but I'll be damned if I'm going to let another woman die on my watch. Oh, and make certain that each patrol denotes the address of warehouses searched. If we're still at this tomorrow, I don't want to be retracing our steps."

Wilson contacted dispatch and made the request for units to be sent to search the warehouse districts still being overhauled, then turned back to talk to Hardwick, "Thirty-six hours isn't a lot of time to wrap up an investigation, especially when it starts in the middle of the night. You and I know that he set us up for failure. It's as if he wants us to fail. As if he wants her to die. Payback for his wife's death, you figure?"

"No, I actually think he wants us to succeed," Hardwick replied thoughtfully. "It's as if he's pushing us to perform at *his* expectations. If he knew how difficult detective work was, he may be of a mind to cut us some slack; but he's a civilian on a mission, and he thinks we should all be brilliant the likes of Sherlock Holmes. Had the police apprehended the killer of his wife quickly, or at all even, he may have accepted the loss and moved on. Something tells me that the murderer got away and now he's running drills on local departments; pushing them to succeed in a shorter span than they normally would."

"Put a man on a clock..."

"...and he runs faster. Precisely," Hardwick confirmed.

Wilson nodded, "Maybe we should include ex- or

current military personnel who lost a loved one in the last decade. If he's running drills..."

Hardwick grinned, but it held no humor, "No, he's too compassionate to be military. If he were military, he'd approach the drills in a more hardened fashion, kill with little-to-no remorse; potentially just shoot them first and inform the police later."

"That's compassionate?" Wilson retorted.

"Absolutely. He may have a shoot-first mentality, but he'd just go after those who kill, not make guiltless people pay for his own suffering. I can't see a military man killing innocent women willy-nilly just to prove a point or accomplish a mission."

"There are those bad apples..."

"We have enough parameters right now without adding speculations on whether we have a bad apple in a bushel of good ones. I'm of a mind that this isn't a military man gone bad."

"Okay, so all we've got to go on, besides the obvious connections, are one killed in a warehouse and one hostage being held in a warehouse district—possibly."

"Yeah, and since there isn't much we can accomplish in the middle of the night, we'll help with the search until morning."

"I know that searching for this latest victim is important, but why am I feeling as if this is a colossal waste of our time?"

"Because we have extraordinarily little to go on? Because we're understaffed and have too much territory to cover? Because we generally work to apprehend a criminal and hope they lead us to their hostage? Instead, we're going about this ass-backwards. What I'd really like to do is head over to her place of employment and interview anyone who knew her, which we'll do as soon as they open their offices," Hardwick stated, pulling into the parking lot of a warehouse in the Castleberry Hill district, where two black and whites were already awaiting their arrival. "I can't shake the feeling that the best way to find Brooke, is to apprehend Price. Maybe Cortez and Harding will turn up something during their computer search that will aid in that," he concluded before climbing from his vehicle.

"We're going to make a sweep of every warehouse in this area," he began without preamble. "Radio in when a sweep is complete, along with the address, so we can make a note and mark it as clear."

"There's a hell of a lot of buildings around here," one of the uniformed officers complained, "and not but six of us."

"Yeah, I know," Hardwick admitted, "but we've got units scouring the other warehouse districts. We're spread thin, but we've got to start our search somewhere. Maybe, come morning, we'll find more information that'll assist in narrowing where we need to focus our resources, but until then, we're going to make full use of the next nine hours. Or do you think your time would be better served sitting back at the station, twiddling your thumbs?"

"We'll start with the buildings on the right," the officer replied curtly, then nodded at his partner to head out.

"I don't think I have to tell you guys to be thorough. Leave no nook or cranny unsearched," Hardwick called after them as they crossed the street. "Okay, Wilson. Let's get this started."

CHAPTER 7

7:30 a.m.

I may be tired, but why are we coming here again? I vaguely remember you mentioning coming over here this morning, but if you wanted to visit the scene of the abduction, couldn't we have done that last night, instead of scouring warehouses—I told you that would be a colossal waste of time, by the way. We barely made any headway," Wilson stated, as they entered the lobby of the Bank of America Plaza. He stifled a yawn and rubbed his face, wishing that he had a cup of coffee to ward off the exhaustion.

"We're not headed to the parking structure. Remember, I said that I wanted to head over to interview

Brooke's employer this morning? Oh, and while you were snoozing on the trip over here, Cortez radioed. Apparently, he found a connection between McIntyre and Madison. They worked together. That's a new lead that can't be overlooked."

"Yeah, I'm simply confused, I guess. I get that interviewing the women's employer may provide valuable intel that might prove useful down the road when we go after Price, but, since we're on a clock, is this really a good use of our time? Although, admittedly, I am kind of glad for the break from scouring warehouses. Do you think it could be a coincidence that the two women worked together? Do you think we could conduct the interviews in the lounge, so we could grab a cup of coffee?"

Hardwick sighed loudly, "We can hold off on the coffee a little longer; as for them working together...it is not coincidental, and you should know that coincidence is just a word of convenience used to overlook facts," Hardwick stated sharply, as he punched the button on the nearest elevator. "I dislike that word immensely. Is anything ever truly coincidental? The two women working together is a fact, and the fact that they worked together presented an opportunity for the perp."

Wilson just shook his head, as the doors slid open to the thirtieth floor. He'd not had the opportunity to respond, nor would he have been able to. He'd been on the police force for eight years, but only made detective grade six months prior. He'd been proud, because making detective grade meant he'd proven himself.

At first, he thought being partnered with Hardwick, a thirty-year veteran, and arguably the most talented detective in Zone 5 of the APD, was the greatest honor of his career; but now, he was tired of being made to feel like a rookie repeatedly. It was as though all the tempering he'd gone through to make detective meant nothing. Of course, he only thought along those lines when Hardwick proved wiser than he was. In reality, he knew that when he'd been on the force as long as Hardwick, he'd likely be just as seasoned, just as capable, and just as smart.

"So, enlighten me?" Wilson asked as they walked toward Brooke's office.

"The fact that the two women worked together and that both were targeted by Price tells you what; aside from the fact that they knew him, which we've already established as highly probable?"

"That he frequented this office and therefore may be known by someone else, who can then point us in his direction?"

"Or he was known by the two women outside of this office, but someone here may know in what capacity, and therefore may be able to point us in his direction," Hardwick quipped.

"Yeah, I can see how this may prove a more valuable lead," Wilson stated, "but we're still aiming our noses toward Price."

"Maybe, but with time moving against us, we need to be where the investigation is most productive without compromising the primary objective—to save Brooke Madison. We have every available officer scouring the warehouses, so it isn't hurting anything for us to be trying to pin down where Price is. If we arrest him, we may be able to compel him to tell us where Brooke is."

Hardwick stopped his explanation and flagged down the first person they encountered when they stepped from the elevator and entered the P.R. Firm of Anderson & Mitchell.

"Excuse me. I'm Detective Hardwick and this is Detective Wilson. We're with the Atlanta PD."

"Here about Brooke?" The older gentleman queried.

"Yes, and Sandra McIntyre."

"Ah, right, Sandra," he acknowledged with a slight shake of his head. "Dear girls—both of them. Always a smile and a kind word. Hard to believe they won't be returning...well, Sandra won't. We can only hope and pray that Brooke will be back soon. I do hope y'all find her and the murdering s.o.b. that took Sandra away." He sighed in sadness. "Follow me. I'll take you to Carissa Anderson. She's the head honcho here. She'll be the one to talk to."

The older man rapped on a closed door and then pushed it open at the muffled "Come in!"

"Detectives, Miss Anderson."

"Are you here about my two employees?" She asked detached, a stiff level of professionalism that had Hardwick wondering if it were a mechanism to ward of stress or sadness. He nodded at her question and tried not to cave to his impulse to give the woman more than a passing glance; something she probably wasn't used to. A quick look at Wilson said he wasn't of the same frame of mind, for he allowed his gaze to roam freely down the length of her tall, lithe form. *That* reaction she was probably more used to. She was the type of woman a man noticed. She was in her late thirties to early forties, but it was apparent that she hit the gym frequently and took care of her health, for her tanned skin glowed, a face devoid of makeup, except for a light application of mascara. He was impressed. She waved a hand at two chairs situated in front of her desk. He cleared his throat and settled onto the high-back chair. It wasn't until she moved to sit that Wilson snapped from his trance and settled onto the other chair.

"I'm not certain how I can help," Carissa began

without preamble. "They worked for me, but I knew little of their personal lives. I certainly don't know of any reason why anyone would want to harm them."

Hardwick sighed inwardly. All too often people rarely felt able or willing to assist because they didn't dwell on the unpleasantness hard enough or long enough to have any recall. People weren't trained to focus on the minute details, so tended to glance over them; forgetting them as soon as a crime scene was cleared, or the local news stopped broadcasting the story.

He, on the other hand, focused continually on small details, and had spent a better part of his career learning how to get others to recall things they might not realize they even knew. He said as much to Carissa. "So, if I can ask you a few questions?" He concluded.

Carissa nodded, the look of uncertainty remaining on her features.

"Did Sandra and Brooke appear to spend a lot of time in conversation, here in the office? Were they friends?" He avoided asking about their after-hours social life, because Carissa had clearly stated she didn't take an interest in her associates outside of work.

Carissa dwelt on the question a considerable time before returning her focus to Hardwick, "If my recollections are correct, I'd say yes. I often spotted them conversing at one or another's desk during work hours."

Hardwick grinned, for he knew what she hadn't included in that statement—that she'd likely reprimanded them for conversing socially during work hours.

"Think back to the past two weeks only," Hardwick continued. "Did you hear them talking about anything in particular? A common interest?"

Carissa immediately started to shake her head, which meant that she wasn't making an effort on this question. Instead of pressing her, he asked another question, "After Sandra's death, did Brooke return to work the next day?"

Carissa nodded.

"Good," Hardwick encouraged. "What was her behavior like?" Did it shift? Her behavior? Besides being sad over the loss, did she do anything different?"

"She was always leery of the parking structure; she had some sort of mild phobia. The next day, though, that phobia changed to an all-out fear. She was in tears when she arrived in the morning, partly over Sandra and partly because of her fear. She said she ran from the car to the elevator, scared senseless that someone would get to her too. Oh God, someone did get to her, and from the same parking structure. Dear Lord, she did have a reason to be afraid..."

"Miss Anderson, try taking a deep breath. We're going to catch this guy, and he's not going to hurt anyone else, okay? Can you keep going?"

"Yes, um, I suggested that she consider seeing a shrink."

"Very good. Believe it or not, that information is important. Since she continued forward, parking where she was uncomfortable, she must have been very brave."

"I'm not certain that bravery had much to do with it. It was the classes that were helping to some extent—I think. Seemed to be, until Sandra...well, Sandra had been taking self-defense classes and had talked Brooke into starting too. I remember, after Sandra was murdered, Brooke commented that she hoped that Christian did a better job..."

"Wait!" Hardwick's head snapped up from his notepad. "Christian? Price?"

"I don't know. I just remember Christian, because of the religious connection."

"May we look through Sandra's desk or Brooke's, please? If we knew where this self-defense place was located..."

"Oh, I can help with that," Carissa commented, then stood and headed out of her office. Since she was walking away, Hardwick made no attempt to hide his appreciation of her form, his gaze pinned to her bottom as he followed her from the office. A nice, rounded, firm bottom he noticed admiringly.

His gaze snapped up when he saw her pivot. She had stopped next to a community bulletin board and had a flyer in her hand. "Sandra posted this last month. I should have taken it down, since it's obvious this Christian fellow was inept at training women to protect themselves, as promised." It was the second tiny crack he witnessed in her polished veneer, which signaled that she wasn't as detached as she wanted everyone to believe.

Wilson collected the flyer, reviewing the simplistic detail:

Defend yourself against predators.
Self-defense for women.
Sign up today @ All Saints' Episcopal Church

"ALL SAINTS'"? Hardwick murmured thoughtfully.

"It's caddy-cornered from here," Carissa volunteered. "Those who were interested in participating in the classes could simply walk over after work. It was a convenient..."

Hardwick interrupted her, "Thank you for your time. If you can think of anything else that may assist in our investigation, please give me a call." He handed her one of his cards and then rushed off towards the row of elevators.

"Think the bishop there might remember Price?" Wilson asked as he raced after Hardwick.

"I'm counting on it, which is why I want you to head to the car first and radio for a sketch artist to meet us at the church a.s.a.p."

"Um, jumping the gun a bit, aren't we? It's possible the bishop won't remember what Price looks like at all. Shouldn't we wait?"

"Since we have less time than I'd care to admit to catch this guy, we don't have the luxury of waiting. I thought I made that clear earlier," Hardwick replied sharply as the elevator slid open.

"I knew that." Wilson sighed and stepped into the elevator.

"As soon as you make the radio call, meet me at the church."

CHAPTER 8

Brooke was oddly grateful that Atlanta was in the middle of a cold snap, which wasn't always the case in October. Still, if it had been the middle of a hot, humid summer night, she'd have suffered a heat stroke attempting to move the heavy refrigerator across the bare concrete flooring. She stopped shoving for a moment to check her progress and had to admit she was surprised. She was more than halfway to the window.

The light filtering through the window told her daylight had arrived, which had her a little concerned. She hadn't realized how long she'd been at it. She glanced at her watch and sucked in a breath of shock. It was already 7:30 a.m. She hadn't made as much progress as she'd first assumed; and at the rate she was going, her time would be up before she even got the fridge beneath the window. According to Christian, she only had until 7:30 a.m. tomorrow in which to be rescued—or to rescue herself.

That caused the anger to set in at the knowledge that she'd have accomplished more in the last several hours and been well on the way to escaping if she'd not shoved too hard on the fridge and tipped it over. It took all of her strength to re-right the appliance. At first, she thought her chances at escape had come to an end, and spent precious hours indulging in tears. Once the tears were spent, she wiped her eyes, smearing her washable mascara. She didn't care about her appearance, but the mascara had gotten in her eyes when she wiped and she sighed in frustration, picking up the edge of her shirt to get the stinging goop out.

The irritation from the mascara worked in concert with her circumstances to elevate her temper and she set about pushing, kicking, and shoving the Kenmore in anger, wasting even more precious time. Eventually, she decided to quit feeling sorry for herself and attempt to lift it back up.

She strained her back and legs slightly in the effort when she hefted the bulky appliance. She managed to push it nearly upright, then quickly scooted beneath it, using her back and legs to right it the rest of the way. If that act of desperation hadn't worked or if she'd slipped, the fridge would have crushed her, and she wouldn't have needed to worry over being killed by Christian or rescued—death would've happened by her own stupidity.

She did succeed in getting the appliance upright however, and after losing more time regaining her breath, she started moving it again, inching it slowly towards her escape route.

"Why did this freakin' room have to be so big," she muttered angrily. As she observed earlier, the room wasn't really that sizable. Perhaps 15x15; however, in Brooke's mind, it was three times that size. "The least he could have done was put the fridge right under the window," she continued her tirade, "to give his victims a fighting chance. Who does he think he is, anyway? How dare he play games with other peoples' lives?" Her foot slid on an oily patch, and she slipped, banging her head on the fridge.

"Son-of-a-bitch!" She screamed, more in frustration at her circumstances than at the actual slip; the pain from which was barely noticeable. She turned and sat, her back against the rusted back panel, and pulled her knees to her chest. She lay her head down on her arms and allowed herself yet another momentary pity party, but one she felt more than entitled to. After she'd exhausted her sorry-for-herself bout, she sniffed loudly, raised her head, and swiped away at the tears.

"I can't give up. I'm not going to let him win. I made it this far, I can make it the rest of the way and still have time to climb out of the window, long before his imposed deadline. I have to." She sniffed again and stood, careful to plant her feet on either side of the barely perceptible slick surface on which she'd slipped. With another heavy sigh, she leaned forward, placed her hands on the sides of the fridge again, and started the same monotonous back-and-forth.

The banging of each movement was oddly rhythmic which triggered a song in Sandra's head. Unfortunately, it happened to be *Oceans Breathe Salty* by Modest Mouse. She stopped pushing for a moment in the hopes of shaking the song from the recesses of her brain, but it clung fast. With deliberate intent, she slowed the pushing of the fridge and started singing the Alphabet Song aloud, keeping perfect rhythm with the swaying of the refrigerator. She felt absurd singing the childish song at the top of her lungs, but anything was better than a song about death, which drove home her own dire circumstances.

From a computer terminal, the man known as Christian Price watched Brooke's attempts with a shake of his head and down-turned lips. He was thankful that she was making an effort and not just sitting back, waiting to die; however, he knew her attempts would prove futile, and he sighed sadly. "Pray they find you, Brooke," he whispered with a quick glance at his stopwatch. "Personally, I have hope this time. This Detective Hardwick seems more competent than cops in other cities."

He returned his gaze to the television, but there weren't any current reports on the APD's progress.

"Well, I think I have time for a Grand Slam at Denny's. I don't believe they'll find her any time soon. Detective Hardwick is good but I've yet to encounter a detective that's *that* good. If any were, women wouldn't die."

CHAPTER 9

Detective Hardwick. May I have a word?" A young African American woman approached as Hardwick and Wilson exited the Bank of America Plaza.

"Not now," Hardwick snapped, as he noticed the camera operator trailing behind, who was apparently, a reporter.

"Detective, I'm Cassandra Bouchard with Channel 5," the woman called, scurrying along behind, "we're live with our viewers and wondered if you have anything to tell them about a report that we received earlier. We've been alerted about an abduction and were told that you only have until seven-thirty a.m. tomorrow morning to locate the victim. Are you close to finding Brooke Madison, or will this guy get away with another murder here in Atlanta, as he did with Sandra McIntyre?"

Hardwick stopped walking abruptly and pivoted sharply, startling the diminutive female.

"Are you ready to comment?" She asked, a bit smugly, placing the microphone beneath Hardwick's nose. He wanted to snatch it from the woman and throw it across the street but knew that would prove poor politics and he didn't fancy being put on administrative leave. Not with a murderer on the loose. Instead, he took a deep breath and released it slowly.

"It would appear that our perp has been in contact with the local media," Hardwick said softly, his tone unpleasant.

"He wanted to ensure that the public lit a fire beneath the Atlanta Police Department's bottoms. He stated that, with a little help, we might just be able to save a woman's life."

"Oh, I'm certain as can be that he appealed to the hearts of everyone at Channel 5."

"Will you find her, Detective?"

"That's our goal, as it always is," Hardwick said and then turned to continue toward the church.

"Well, we'll be with you every step of the way," the reporter stated, following again. When it looked as if

Hardwick might complain, she added, "We won't get in your way. After all, we all want this man caught and Brooke Madison freed."

As soon as Hardwick entered the church, the reporter faced the camera, "This is Cassandra Bouchard reporting live, currently outside All Saints' Episcopal Church, here on Peachtree Street, where the APD's Detective Hardwick is following up a lead on the kidnapping of Atlanta native, Brooke Madison. People are urged to remain vigilant and report anything, which may assist detectives in locating this missing woman. We'll continue to monitor the situation and bring you updates, as they happen."

Hardwick wasn't amused at having a reporter on his heels and was fuming as he entered the church's vestibule. Despite his anger, he had to admit that he may need to use them in this investigation, so holding his temper in check would be to his benefit.

He spotted a door with "Bishop's Office" on it, and headed that way, his stride long and determined. He knocked sharply and turned the knob without waiting for an invitation to enter. It was locked, which made him even more irate. He wanted to ram his shoulder into it, just to let off steam. Instead, he started counting to ten repeatedly, breathing in and out of his nostrils.

He was about to search the rest of the church, when

he heard someone on the other side of the door, turning the knob.

An aging African American man wearing a jogging suit exited, "What I can do for you?" He asked politely, rubbing sleep from his eyes.

"I'm sorry if I woke you, Bishop," Hardwick stated, suddenly aware that he didn't really expect to find the bishop at the church at this hour of the morning, but here he was, and appeared to have slept in his office. Well, that couldn't concern him at present. "I'm Detective Hardwick, APD," he said tersely, showing the bishop his badge. "I'm investigating two murders that have occurred in the last week."

"Murder? Well, that's something new here in Atlanta?" The priest replied with a sarcastic tone that bespoke of too many years watching people in the neighborhood die—slain by ex-lovers, gang members, or other equally stupid reasons. "That explain the news reporter hounding you outside? When I saw the news van, I was about to turn on the tv to see what's happening."

"Yeah, it's definitely all over the news. Anyway, a man going by the name of Christian Price used this church to offer self-defense classes to women in the surrounding businesses," he explained, handing the flyer to the bishop.

"Yes, I am aware," he stated and then his eyes grew

wider, "Christian?" The bishop queried incredulous. "You think Christian was behind these heinous crimes?"

"We don't think it, we know it," Hardwick replied harshly, rashly. "He used the self-defense class as a way of singling out his potential victims and now he's given us a very narrow window in which to locate and save his latest victim, Brooke Madison."

"Brooke Madison," the bishop said sadly. "She attended church here. An extremely sweet girl, however, I don't know how I can be of help. I haven't seen Christian in a few days." The priest shook his head, "I've been at this church for nigh onto forty years and think I've seen everything, but just when I think I have, somebody throws shock in my face and knocks me for a loop. I never would have thought that that man would hurt a flea."

"Well, it appears he has and since you know him, I have a sketch artist on the way. I need you to provide a likeness for that news reporter outside. We will do everything we can to save Brooke; but we also need to catch the man you know as Christian Price before he does this to someone else. You can help us do that."

"I'll certainly do what I can," the bishop replied, nodding solemnly. "I'm sure you hear this a lot, but he doesn't seem the sort to kill people. He was a new member to the congregation. Immensely helpful with the elderly ladies. Seemed a likeable fellow; so, when he approached and said that he was trained in martial arts and would love to rent space in the basement to teach ladies to defend themselves..."

"He paid the rent in cash, I assume?"

"No, I actually didn't charge him anything in the end, him doing the community a service and all."

"I know that it's probably too much to ask, but you wouldn't happen to have an address on file for this man, would you? Or just know where he lives, by chance?"

The bishop shook his head, the frown on his face deepening, "Providing an address is completely optional by members of the congregation. Not a lot of people do nowadays. I guess they don't want religious nuts knocking on their doors. Most religious visitations, unless requested, have been relegated to that of a nuisance solicitation. Sad times we live in."

"I figured it might be a long shot, but I had to ask," Hardwick sighed. Just then, Wilson strolled in with another police officer following closely.

"Bishop, this is our resident artist, Officer Mitchell. He'll help you put together a likeness of Christian Price."

The bishop nodded and waved toward his office, "If you want to set your laptop up on my desk, officer, I'll join you in a moment."

"Sure thing," Mitchell said, and moved past the bishop.

"Oh, and Mitchell," Hardwick called, "give that sketch to the reporter outside when it's done and printed, okay? She *is* still outside, isn't she, Wilson?"

Wilson nodded.

When the business with Mitchell concluded, Hardwick turned back to the priest, "Something else on your mind, Bishop?"

"I'm not sure, but I just recollected something. Might be helpful, I don't know," the bishop said, rubbing his face.

"I'll take anything right now, Bishop," Hardwick admitted.

The bishop nodded, "I seem to recall that Price called me late last week, seemed deep in his cups. Ranting about how the police had let him down when his wife was murdered. He rambled on a bit, and then I asked if he needed me to call him a cab so he could get home safely from where he was at."

"And where was that?"

"He said he was at The Tavern at Phipps Plaza."

"And did you call him a cab?"

The bishop shook his head, "No, he said that I wasn't to worry. He could walk home from there."

Hardwick nodded, suddenly feeling a surge of

renewed energy flow through his body. Knowing a particular area in which a suspect might be located was like someone handing him a much-anticipated present for Christmas—in this case, that present was the potential of a speedy arrest. "Thank you, Bishop. You've been a great help."

The bishop walked toward his office and Hardwick rubbed the back of his neck, trying desperately to reduce the tension building in his muscles. Even though the likelihood of arresting Price was getting closer each passing minute; until it happened, the tension would not diminish.

Wilson seemed to know instinctively that Hardwick was thinking about hunting down the perp. "It wouldn't be a good use of time to search the residential area around The Tavern, any more than searching every single warehouse in the Atlanta area, you know that, right? That area is enormous."

Hardwick nodded, "Yeah, that would seem to be an accurate assessment, with so many houses and too many apartment complexes; however, it's currently the best lead we have for catching this guy and we'd be remiss to overlook it, wouldn't you agree?"

"Not really. It would take days to do a complete sweep of the area, as you well know," Wilson countered.

"And by then Brooke will be long dead, and he'll have

had plenty of opportunity to find another victim. Not being able to catch him *now* makes me want to ram my fist into something," Hardwick snapped.

"As long as it isn't my face," Wilson quipped. "Besides, we have every cop scouring the warehouses searching for our victim. It wouldn't do any good to pull any of them to try a search of the apartments around The Tavern..."

Hardwick sighed, "Yeah, it would be futile. We'll distribute the drawing when it's done. See if that presents any viable leads. We'll postpone a search of Price for now, since I must concede that locating him can't be our priority. Not with so little time given to find the victim."

"So now where?" Wilson asked as they exited the church. A glance at his watch revealed the hour to be after 8 a.m. He didn't like how fast time flew when a deadline was in place.

Hardwick didn't answer, rather headed to where the reporter was speaking to her camera operator, "Miss Bouchard?"

Cassandra jumped and instinctively pointed to her camera operator to begin filming, but Detective Hardwick waved him away, "We don't have anything for you, but we will in about half hour or so. We have an officer inside generating a sketch of the possible suspect. We want you to air his likeness during one of your live feeds. Can you do that?"

"Of course."

"It's much appreciated. The more help we have in finding this guy, the more chance there is to prevent Brooke Madison's death. It wouldn't hurt to ask people to be on the lookout for him."

"Absolutely. So, where are you two going now? Do you have another lead to follow up on?"

"Yes, but if you'll stay here and wait for that likeness?"

"I will."

"I admit to not being fond of news reporters," Hardwick stated, "but this is one time where having you nearby may prove beneficial."

Cassandra grinned wryly, "Well, I never thought I'd ever hear you say that Detective Hardwick, but it has certainly made my morning."

Hardwick smiled in reply and then waved at Wilson. They headed back to Hardwick's car. "Recommendations?" Hardwick asked, cruising along Peachtree Street.

"I feel we should go back to assisting with a search of the warehouses, to help the units on patrol right now; but I confess to feeling a bit small and uncertain that we can make a dent, but we aren't likely to find Price first..." Wilson started with a sigh, then stopped.

"Which is why we're not doing this alone, remember?"

"Yeah, I know. It just feels like it."

"Any way for you to pull up warehouse locations on my laptop?" Hardwick asked, pointing to beneath the passenger seat. "That way I don't feel as if we're just driving around blind."

Wilson reached beneath his seat and pulled out the case, "I don't know if such a listing exists, but I agree to not wanting to drive around without a purpose. It would make me feel as if I were trying to climb a mountain with my hands tied behind my back."

"Definitely not a good feeling," Hardwick concurred, "so, let's see about making things a little easier by mapping out those warehouse locations, then we won't feel as if we're running around directionless. Obviously eliminate the primary locations that we started on last night. That was a jumping off point, but by no means proved a comprehensive search."

"Don't you think the captain would have units patrolling other warehouse locations? We're just as likely to overlap with other black and whites as to do any good."

"Right. Okay, localize your search. See if you find a listing of warehouses anywhere near Phipps Plaza.

Maybe if Price is drinking around there and is in walking distance, he may be stashing his victims near there. It's thin on logic, but it's better than starting nowhere."

CHAPTER 10

Brooke was exhausted, and self-pitying tears ran unchecked down her cheeks. Moving a refrigerator may be an easy task for a man, but for someone of her four-foot-eight petite stature, she may as well be trying to move Mount Rushmore.

Still, as the hours ticked by, she did make progress; although it was far slower than she'd have preferred. She gauged the distance between where it currently was to the wall beneath the window...so close, but the gap was still too far from the wall. She sat down with her back against the fridge door, place her hands on the ground, pulled her knees up to provide the needed leverage, and then shoved as hard as she could. A moment later it bumped to a stop. She stood and wiped her hands on her shirt, pleased that this part of her work was completed. Now she just needed to reach that window.

At this point, she wasn't wasting any more of her precious time. She judged the top of the fridge to be about a foot and a half taller than herself. She stood on her tiptoes and latched onto the rusty edge. "I'm going to need a tetanus shot if I get cut," she moaned, and then attempted to pull her weight up. She wasn't a weakling, but after struggling with a fridge for hours, her arms muscles were shuddering with fatigue. After a few minutes of exertion, not accomplishing a thing, she let her arms and legs drop, and screamed in frustration at the top of her lungs. Tears pricked her eyes again and she suddenly had the urge to give up and wait for the police to free her. She was sick and tired of being tired; was even sicker of feeling helpless and crying as if hormonal.

The thought of sitting and doing nothing jarred her from her pity party and she shook away the feeling of helplessness. Time was ticking away fast. She had less than twenty hours remaining. It seemed a long time, but so had the time she'd spent moving the fridge—it seemed forever until it wasn't. The thought that she wouldn't be able to climb up to the window and out to freedom fast enough, had her nerves jumping, producing a rush of adrenaline, and a renewed determination. She would get to that window or die trying. She certainly wasn't going to sit on her haunches waiting on someone else to rescue her. She returned to her tiptoes, reached up and latched hold again.

"Please," she whispered, and immediately put her feet against the side panel, pulling with all her might as her toes shimmied up the side. Within minutes, she topped the old green Kenmore. She immediately noticed the rusted, pitted surface and carefully moved about until she could sit without falling through the surface.

She released a sigh of relief, "Me, two, Christian... well, he's still got the advantage, but I'm about to change *that*! I'm getting out of here—as soon as my body stops quaking."

After ten minutes and with exaggerated care, she moved to a standing position and her hope again waned. Two things made this endeavor potentially undoable.

The first was the condition of the top, which she wish she'd known about before making the effort to use the fridge as an escape tool. Still, she was up here now, so she just needed to move about gingerly. She shifted her feet to the sides, but that stance shaved a couple of inches from her height, which brought her mind to bear on her second issue—the height to the window.

That window was far higher than she'd first estimated. She did a quick mental calculation. The fridge was approximately seventy inches high. She was a diminutive fifty-six inches high, minus two inches for her widened stance, which put her at one-hundred-twenty-four inches from the floor. A little over ten feet. She craned her neck and decided that it was a twenty-foot ceiling, which meant the window was situated about eight feet above her head. She wasn't going to make that by leaping.

Eight feet.

She sighed loudly, "Dear sweet Jesus, how in the name of all that's holy am I going to make that distance? There's got to be some way."

She examined the brick wall carefully, noting the uneven lay of the bricks and the many areas in which the concrete in between had deteriorated and crumbled away, leaving more than enough crannies to latch onto. She glanced down at her feet, size five; and then imagined her tiny toes gripping the bricks.

"Would it be possible?" It was risky, but so was waiting here to die. She reached up beneath her skirt and tugged the hose down, slipping them off carefully, so she didn't teeter off the side of the small surface she was standing on.

"There, now there's nothing between me and those nooks," she observed, but still hesitated in starting the climb. It wasn't that she thought herself incapable, but one false move and she could take a serious tumble, one that could break bone. She sighed heavily.

"Just pretend you're rock climbing and don't dwell on the fact that you've never rock-climbed a day in your life. Think only of freedom."

She took a deep breath and let it out with a whoosh, then reached up to the nearest hole that she was certain her fingers could latch onto and then positioned her foot on one closer to where she stood. It was an experimental start; to ensure that she'd be able to pull her weight up the wall. She tugged her body upward and remained suspended there for a few seconds and then lowered herself back down. She drew in a deep steadying breath.

"Okay, it's doable, and as this looks to be my only solution for escaping...here I go."

CHAPTER 11

Nov 1st, 6:30 a.m.

G ood morning, Atlanta, and welcome to the six-thirty edition of Channel 5 news. I'm Patricia Wheaton.

And I'm Charles Braxton. This hour marks a deadline rapidly closing in for our men in blue.

That's right, Charles. On the evening before Halloween, we were notified by an anonymous source that Atlanta resident, Brooke Madison, had been abducted, and her assailant had given local police only thirty-six hours in which to locate the victim or she would die. As of this morning, police have only one hour to reach that deadline.

It certainly is tense, Patricia, especially as all eyes are currently on the Atlanta Police Department at this hour, who *are scouring every inch of every warehouse in the Atlanta district.*

Channel 5 correspondent, Tanya Marks, has been following social media to get a feel for local response to this crisis. Tanya?

Thank you, Patricia. Since we first aired this story yesterday morning, social media sites have been bombarded with comments regarding this incident. Some people who know Brooke have been sending prayers and messages of hope to her family, while others are urging police to do their job and find her. One post, however, has received a multitude of responses, some supportive and others condemning the comment as callous. The post was by screen name I am de man.

I am de man *writes: "What makes this woman so special?"*

Christian's gaze shot up from the computer monitor and he grinned, listening intently.

He goes on to write: "Men, women, and children of Atlanta, and in other cities, die daily, yet they receive no notice. The police make only a half effort to locate their killer but put the police on a clock and shine the light of media on them, and suddenly it appears that they have a heart and genuinely care. Why is that? Why can't they treat every missing person's case, every burglary, or every homicide with the same due diligence?"

"They can't even catch clues when they are thrown right into their faces," Christian said sardonically, looking at the screen name he'd created in which to write that post. Using *I Am De Man* had been a brash in-your-face, out-of-character move for him; but he was sincerely tired of killing. Tired of his attempts to light a fire beneath local law enforcement failing. With Detective Hardwick on this case, he naively believed he'd be leaving Atlanta with only one kill; that Brooke would be spared; that he'd be marking this city off his list in which he needed to conduct experiments.

He sighed loudly and returned his attention to the monitor, watching as Brooke made a pathetic attempt to scale a brick wall. She'd stopped and restarted several times by his calculations over the course of the day yesterday, each time gaining a slighter higher distance on the wall before giving up and moving back down, only to rest for a short bit before trying again. He winced, wondering when she'd drop off the wall and straight off the fridge onto the concrete floor, or crash through the top. He shuddered at that thought. He knew it was likely that her life would be forfeit in about an hour; however, that didn't mean he wouldn't care about her wellbeing until then. He did feel for her efforts, knowing they were costing her a lot—both in energy and damage to her flesh. He couldn't see her fingers or toes, but as many times as she'd started up and down the wall, he knew that those digits had to be raw by now, bleeding. And if that wasn't bad enough, her muscles had to be screaming in agony from the attempts to hold on to a surface that wasn't meant to be held onto.

During the entire day, yesterday, he'd watch as she tested her confidence and ability to shimmy up a wall—like Spiderman, minus the special abilities. She would climb as far as she thought able, look down at her progress, then slowly return. He didn't know why she always stopped and scooted down instead of pushing through the agony and continuing to the window. He could only surmise that she stopped when she felt her grip giving way and felt it better to scoot back down and rest than lose that grip and crash.

It wasn't until around 11 p.m. last night that exhaustion, or the realization surrounding her circumstances, finally overtook her and she stopped her attempts. She slid off the top of the fridge and moved to the bed, sitting down heavily. She drew her knees up and lie her head down. At first, with the rise and fall of her shoulders, he thought she was crying silently; but soon after, she tilted sideways, fell onto her side, and then stretched out fully. She'd fallen asleep.

He was certain that was the end of her attempts, but around 4 a.m. she woke with a start, stretched, and climbed back atop the fridge, as if prompted by an unseen force. He wanted to tell her to patiently wait on the police; that they were scheduled to rescue her within a few hours, but he could not fault her wanting to try to save herself. If it were he in her position, he'd be doing the same. After all, anyone with a lick of common sense knew not to rely too heavily on local law enforcement. They were simply overworked and undermanned, or too apathetic.

He shook his head and cringed when she reached for the wall then withdrew with a sharp inhalation. She stood examining her appendages, confirming his suspicions that trying to scale a brick wall was hurting her. Still, he was impressed. Not many women he'd encountered had the fight in them that she did. It made him will the police to find her even more. This was one woman that deserved to live.

She started determinedly back up the wall, pushing past the pain, and had been at it for the better part of the early morning. He turned his gaze away from the monitor and glanced at the stopwatch on the desk next to him, the seconds ticking away. The police now had less than forty-five minutes left in which to locate her. After an entire day-and-a-half of searching, he doubted they would succeed now.

A piercing scream rent the air and he jerked his gaze back to the monitor, watching with macabre interest as Brooke lost her grip from halfway up the brick wall and crashed through the rusted top of the Kenmore. The screaming continued, though the tone had changed from one of fear to one of agony. Although he could no longer see her, he easily envisioned her inside the old fridge, one- or both legs broken.

"Oh, my dear Brooke, it would appear you must rely on the police to save you after all, although I wouldn't hold out hope. I know *I've* given up hope, which is why it's time for me to start considering my next victim. Don't worry though, my dear. I'll be here until the very end. Perhaps you'll pass out from the shock and die peacefully unconscious. It's always my preference that my victims be awake at the end, but for you…well, I wish unconsciousness. You've suffered enough."

With a heavy sigh, he stood. It was time to start cleaning up his gear and getting set to leave. His faith in Hardwick and the Atlanta P.D. may have waned, but his faith in technology was still very high, and he knew that once he placed that final call to inform them of Brooke's whereabouts, they'd start a trace. He didn't know whether tracing a burner cell was even possible with current technology, but it wasn't a risk he was willing to take.

He gave a quick glance at his stopwatch. He'd be making that call in thirty minutes, which meant that before he finalized tear down, he needed to do one final thing. He clicked a button on his computer, which activated the speaker he'd set up inside the warehouse, "If you're awake, I just want you to know I'm sorry for your pain, Brooke, but you won't have to endure for much longer now."

CHAPTER 12

Nov 1st, 7:25 a.m.

Nothing? The patrols have found nothing?" Hardwick yelled in frustration, slamming his hands against the steering wheel.

"And neither have we," Wilson said, stifling a yawn. Given more time, he knew that Hardwick would have found the girl and have caught the perp too. He had a good record for closing cases. He was one of the reasons that crime in Zone 5 remained low; but the pressure of being thrust into a race against time was more than his psyche could bear.

The radio squawked and both men became more

alert. Hardwick snatched at the receiver, "Go for Hardwick."

Hardwick, this is Cortez. I thought you should know that my research turned up something interesting. It would appear that our man, Christian Price, has been very busy up and down the east coast. In five cities, that I've discovered thus far, there have been twenty murders with a similar M.O., in which the perp has given police a time limit in which to locate his victims. Sometimes thirty-six hours, sometimes as little as twelve hours. Police didn't make a connection because of the diversity of the time limits and the types of kills. Now, get this. In each instance, as the number of kills increased, he's assisted the police almost to the point of absurdity; providing everything but the actual location, so that the police could swoop in and save the day. Only when a victim was rescued, did this guy stop his "experiments".

"He went by the name Christian Price?"

No. In some cases, he didn't provide a name. In others, he used a different name altogether.

"So, he's very interested in us finding and saving his victims, but he's less eager to be found himself."

Considering what's he'd done, I can't say as...uh oh.

"What, what is it?" Wilson asked, but a quick glance at the clock told them both why Cortez had made that outburst. It was seven-thirty a.m. Time was up.

Over the radio, Hardwick and Wilson heard the

phone ring and Hardwick closed his eyes in despair, waiting.

This is Detective Cortez

After a short pause, Cortez continued, *no, Detective Hardwick is out on patrol. I can patch you through.*

Another short pause followed and then Cortez came back on the radio.

You know whose calling, Hardwick, so I'll put him through to you.

Hardwick drew in a deep breath and released it quickly, "We need to run a trace."

Already started.

"Okay. I'll do what I can to keep him talking." He took another deep breath and then told Cortez to connect the caller. "This is Detective Hardwick."

I held out such high hopes for you, the caller said softly, but that didn't lessen the anger emanating from his tone.

"You're a murdering son of a bitch, and I'll see you hang for this," Hardwick retorted, his breathing heavy. "Tell me where she is!" He demanded. "There's still time for us to get to her. You don't have to kill her."

Christian sniffed loudly, then responded in a tone devoid of emotion, *you will find Brooke at 565 Northside Drive, SW. Dispatch an ambulance also. If she is still alive, she will need serious medical attention. And Detective, I suggest you allow your men to take some time off. We'll start again later.*

Before Hardwick could snap another response, the connection went dead.

"Radio Cortez back," He commanded, accelerating toward Northside Drive.

"We're only a few miles from there," Wilson said softly, picking up the microphone.

"Yeah," Hardwick responded. "Too close. Atlanta is simply too big a city; too many places to hide someone. We could have come upon it eventually, but not necessarily at all. Give Cortez the address and don't forget that ambulance."

A quick glance in his rearview showed the Channel 5 truck, following along behind him. They'd not left his vicinity since last night. He'd hope, beyond hope, that releasing a sketch of Christian Price would see the man in custody, but he'd avoided detection; and now a woman was dead, or was soon to be, and he was going to have to explain to that very media why he'd failed. It was something he wasn't used to. He was used to catching the bad guys and saving the innocent victims.

As he squealed to a stop, he barely threw his car into park before leaping out. Cassandra Bouchard exited her car just as fast and came racing along after him, her cameraman hot on her heels.

"Detective," she shouted, sprinting up to Hardwick, microphone extended, "we've just received a phone call that another woman will be kidnapped tomorrow. Do you have a comment on that, or why the entire police force was unable to locate Brooke Madison before the perpetrator released a deadly gas that killed her?"

CHAPTER 13

After a long while, Brooke finally stopped screaming, though the pain in her leg was more than she'd suffered in her entire life. She glanced down at the bone protruding from her calf muscle and started crying.

She reached out and attempted to shove open the refrigerator door, but the movement caused a sharp, unbearable agony to ricochet throughout every nerve in her body and she screamed again. Had she realized that the latch to the old fridge locked automatically from the outside when closed, she could have saved herself the effort and the agony. It was a design flaw in the older style refrigerators. Had she been shut up in a newer model, she may have been able to prevent a more rapid end to her life.

"If you're awake, I want you to know that I'm sorry for your pain, Brooke," a voice interjected into her anguish, "but you won't have to endure for much longer now."

"Christian, please, let me go," Brooke yelled, her voice choked with tears. "I'm hurt really bad. Isn't that enough suffering for one person to have to go through? Surely my life isn't worth taking just because I wasn't your star pupil."

"Do you really think this has to do with you?" Christian sighed loudly.

"Of course, it has to do with me, or is there actually someone else inside this refrigerator, and I'm simply unconscious somewhere having a terrifying out-of-body, very realistic experience!" She screamed.

There was no reply, only several faint whirring sounds, followed closely by loud hissing sounds, which lasted for more than five minutes. Shortly after, the rancid odor of bitter almonds reached her nostrils and she cringed.

"It's 7:25 a.m. now, Brooke. If you're fortunate, and the police arrive before the given deadline of 7:30, you may not suffer any long-term effects from the concentrated dose of Hydrogen Cyanide which released a few minutes ago. At 7:30, if they haven't broken through the door, I'll notify the police of your whereabouts, so to give you a fighting chance. Believe me, I'm rooting for a speedy arrival, and a happy ending. As promised, I'll stay with you until the end."

Brooke wanted to pose a response but couldn't. She felt overwhelmingly dizzy and nauseated. Her eyes stung and she was having more difficulty drawing a breath that didn't burn her lungs. A memory of her chemistry class flittered into the forefront of her mind and she knew she was dead, for Hydrogen Cyanide was the same chemical the Germans had used in World War II to commit mass murder.

She tried to prepare herself for the potential symptoms she was likely to face, but only listed a couple before another symptom manifested: loss of consciousness.

CHAPTER 14

7:40 p.m.

Hardwick and Wilson stormed into the warehouse on Northside Drive, and immediately began kicking in doors of the rooms lining the main hall. They kicked open the door of the room where Brooke was being held and immediately fell back as the Hydrogen Cyanide escaped, assaulting the detectives eyes and throat as brutally as an assailant with an Uzi.

Hardwick reached in and pulled the door closed rapidly, knowing that there was no way they'd be able to reach Brooke now—not before the gas killed her. They weren't even going to be able to enter to search for her, not without putting their own lives at risk.

Hardwick kicked the wall, then turned on Wilson, grinding out the next instructions between his clenched teeth, "Get back to the radio and call in the hazmat unit. Inform them of the situation and ask that they arrive in all haste."

Wilson nodded and then bolted back out the way they'd come.

Hardwick slid down the wall and sat, waiting. He was supremely angry—over the loss of Brooke Madison, over the feelings of incompetence welling inside his chest, but especially at Christian Price.

"When I find him, his life is forfeit," he murmured, just as the hazmat team arrived. Hardwick glanced at his watch—8 a.m. It had only taken the hazmat unit fifteen minutes to assemble and arrive, but it was still too long. Next time—and he knew there'd be a next time—he would ensure that all departments were on standby and ready to act on a moment's notice.

The hazmat team worked quickly to expel all traces of the gas, so that the detectives could begin their search; however, that took another half hour, so that it was nearing 8:30 a.m. by the time the sergeant in charge of the hazmat unit declared it safe to enter.

"We didn't see any signs of her while we worked to clear the gas," the unit chief announced. "Maybe this wasn't the location..."

"It's got to be the location," Hardwick interjected.

He and Wilson, along with a half dozen uniformed officers entered with alacrity, but a quick sweep turned up no trace of Brooke's body, and for a short instance, Hardwick and Wilson thought that they'd caught a break; that Christian had merely sent them on a wild goose chase and that Brooke was alive and well in another building across town.

That relief was short-lived when a uniformed officer opened the refrigerator and called out, "Here! She's here!"

CHAPTER 15

Hardwick sank wearily onto the chair at his desk and started typing up the report on both Sandra McIntyre and Brooke Madison. Now that he knew that there was a connection, he could add the necessary details and combine both files. He realized, however, that there would be another body added to the file soon, if he and his fellow detectives didn't find the next person abducted by Price—when he got around to abducting her, that is. The more he realized that the end wasn't in sight, the angrier he got, until he was fairly beating on the keys.

"Shouldn't we be out searching for Price?" Wilson asked, as he watched Hardwick type aggressively on his keyboard. "If we catch him, he can't abduct any more women; and we'll close the book on at least two dozen murder cases; and you're about to punch a hole in that keyboard."

Hardwick started to respond, but his gaze fell on the image of Cassandra Bouchard on the television monitor in the captain's office. She was standing in front of the abandoned warehouse reporting, no doubt, on the incompetence of the APD. He watched, with renewed dismay, as paramedics carried the black bag, holding Brooke Madison's body, to a waiting hearse. The coroner had pronounced her dead at the scene.

Bouchard had attempted to question him as Wilson and he left the warehouse, but he'd rushed to his car and drove directly back to his precinct. He couldn't see himself justifying his incompetence. Not right now. Right now, he just needed to return to his cave to lick his wounds.

As the image of Bouchard faded and returned to the two anchors manning the Channel 5 desk, the anticipated wave of the captain's hand came. Hardwick stood slowly, "Let's go get this over with, Wilson. Cortez, Harding, you may as well sit in on this meeting." He headed over, his legs feeling as if they were filled with concrete.

All four men filed into the captain's office, expressions dejected, but the anticipated ass-chewing didn't happen.

"It's going to happen again," the captain softly, worry in his tone. "Just before I waved you in here, the news agency stated that Price called them a few minutes prior, saying that he would definitely be abducting another woman, and that he was giving the local police department one more chance to prove some level of competency."

"Well, isn't that just thoughtful of him," Harding snapped sarcastically.

"Any word yet from the other Zone Commanders, on a willingness to offer some assistance?" Hardwick asked, trying to keep the frustration in his tone at a minimum.

The captain nodded, "I received word from every one of them, offering their condolences on landing this nut job in our precinct; but, as anticipated, they feel they have too many of their own head cases to deal with, without adding ours to their agendas. Quite frankly, they're only glad they aren't the focus of this madman or the media. They also feel this is a political time bomb, so are reluctant to offer any support that's going to draw attention to their own precincts."

"What a bunch of dicks," Wilson snapped.

"Politics at its best," Cortez muttered.

"Give me something, Hardwick," the captain moaned.

"I've got the commissioner and the mayor breathing down my neck now. Tell me you've got something that I can give them. A lead on this guy's whereabouts? Anything?"

He and Wilson exchanged glances at the request of a location, but before Wilson could throw them under the bus on why they didn't pursue that information, Cortez piped up, "We can give the press the information we have right now on Price's former victims," Cortez volunteered. "That will give them a focus other than our own asses."

"What information?"

"Hardwick had me start an immediate search for Price's other victims," Cortez started.

"What made you think there were others?" The captain interrupted.

"A conversation that Price and I had just before we started the investigation."

"I really need to read the reports more frequently," the captain muttered. "So, this guy's done this before?"

"In five other states that I've located thus far; and there have been at least twenty other victims. We give that information to the press, and they'll run with it. They'll be doing so much investigative work on their own, that they may even tell us something we overlooked. It'll also make us look less incompetent, because it'll show that the deadlines are impossible and that other police precincts had the same difficulties, despite putting their best men on the job," Cortez concluded.

"Okay, bring me the data and I'll contact the press."

Cortez left the office and the captain turned back to address the remaining three officers, "Okay, onto other business. Has the lab been able to find any trace on the camera or the canister left at the scene?"

"There hasn't been enough time for the lab to find any trace evidence. They've been advised that it's a rush," Wilson answered. "You know what I don't get? That was a wireless remote camera, which means there had to be a Wi-Fi signal in use from somewhere, but that's an old warehouse, not one that's been revamped yet..."

"It was a wireless camera, as you mentioned, Wilson. To use it, he would simply need to be..."

"He was nearby!" Cortez interjected angrily. *"¡Ay Dios, Santa Maria!"*

"Not necessarily," Hardwick said, shaking his head. "There are Wi-Fi boosters that can extend a signal a fair distance from the source. Either way, his location makes no difference. The fact that he managed to set up so elaborately tells us he's highly educated and skilled...in electronics and chemicals."

"Okay, how can that help us?" The captain queried.

"If there were a serial number on any of the equipment left at the scene, we maybe could run a trace on it. Get a better ID on the guy," Wilson replied dejected. "But he didn't just file it off, which may have been reversible —at least according to a Bones episode I watched." Wilson blushed at the looks aimed his way and cleared his throat, "Sorry. Anyway, if he had filed them off, it may have been possible to read the serial numbers still, but he didn't; he removed them in a way that has left it impossible to retrieve."

"Okay, since he removed identifiable markings, we can assume that he's also familiar with forensics," Hardwick added.

"Great, we're dealing with a Kim Ung-Yong," the captain quipped sarcastically.

"Who?" Harding asked.

"One of the smartest geeks on the planet, with an IQ of around 210," Hardwick replied instinctively.

"Sorry," the captain apologized, "I know that wasn't helpful. So, this guy, Price, he monitors the area with a camera. When his deadline is reached, he releases a chemical agent into the room via…"

"It was set on a timer," Hardwick responded. "Our techs say it was set so that the timer cancelled if the door was breached by whatever time Price designated. If the door remained closed, the countdown went to zero and activated the release of the gas. He didn't have to be anywhere near the location to know what was happening; to know whether Brooke lived or died."

The captain sighed heavily, "Okay, so do we have any idea on how to approach the next abduction? How do we go about finding her without wasting manpower on all-out searches? This city is simply too big to conduct effective sweeps; and if he places her outside of our particular jurisdiction, we'll really be up shit creek."

"There isn't anything we can do different, Captain, other than alert hazmat to be ready at a moment's notice and continue to work around the clock," Hardwick replied. "Unless he gives us better clues, there isn't a damned thing we can do. We followed the leads we had, but they were pointing more toward finding Price than the victim."

"What do you mean, finding Price," the captain queried with a heavy knit in his brow. "You mean, we had the opportunity to stop..."

"No," Hardwick interjected quickly. "We were only following up leads..."

"...and the primary lead," Wilson jumped in, not wanting his partner to take the full brunt of the captain's wrath; especially since the decision not to pursue was equally his fault, "didn't guarantee an arrest."

Hardwick sighed and picked up the explanation, "The

priest gave us a hint, a nibble, as to an area in which we might locate Price."

"But the area was too sizable, much like the search for the warehouse," Wilson continued. "It wouldn't have been prudent to split our search teams. We needed all men looking for Brooke."

"Okay, I get it, but now we have quite a bit of leeway before Price's next abduction..."

"That we know of," Hardwick interjected. "For all we know, he could the call within the next hour."

"Fine, if the call comes in, we recall all units, but until then, we have some time. What can we do with it?"

"I'm not certain it will be effective because it would mean doing another all-out sweep of the residential zones around The Tavern at Phipps Plaza; and that's assuming that he's still lying low in a place around that area. He could've moved on. If not, what can we do? We'd have to call in all black and whites to accomplish a search that extensive, and not a one of them have slept in over thirty-six hours. Still, with the sketch we got from the bishop, we'd definitely have a better shot at getting Price into custody than locating an abductee at this point."

"Searching for Price is better than sitting around doing nothing while he plans another abduction. So, let's get the sketch to every patrol's on-board computer," the captain snapped, "and have officers start an immediate sweep. I want each area in each grid closed during the search. No one enters or departs until cleared. Put the men on rotations. I know we're short-handed, but the officers aren't going to be any good to anyone if they crash a patrol car or overlook something vital. Half on patrol, half on mandatory rest here at the precinct. Two-hour rotations."

All three men nodded as Cortez came back carrying a file for the captain containing all the other potential victims linked to Price. "I'll take care of getting this to the press; you take care of the other," the captain said, picking up the receiver to dial the local media.

CHAPTER 16

P rice tilted his head and listened to the sirens in the distance. He judged them to be some distance away, yet instinctively knew that the police were searching for him. That angered him, but he knew he couldn't allow that anger to control his actions. He took several deep breaths and then continued packing up his computer gear. If not for the search, he may have been able to utilize this apartment for his next abduction. Having to locate a new place to monitor from, set up for the experiment, and finding another unwilling participant for his experiment would take more time than he wanted; but he couldn't get caught.

He cocked his head, listening carefully, judging how far away the patrol cars were. The further away they remained, the longer he had to clear out his equipment. The one thing he couldn't do was rush. Rushing meant overlooking something, and when he left a location, he left it as clean as if no one lived there. He knew that was suspicious in itself, but since the occupant generally had no recollection of the time he was there, he or she generally had no recollection of the condition of their living quarters either. He knew that those individuals he stayed with would waken in a fog of lost time; could always report that lost time to the police, but there wouldn't be anything linking them to him. That's because he always chose those people as carefully as he did his victims. In this case, he'd selected to stay with Consuela from his martial arts class because she'd mentioned starting a vacation this week, which meant she wouldn't be missed.

Price also felt less rushed because not only were the police a fair distance away by the sounds of their sirens, but also because he had set up in a densely packed apartment complex, so even if they arrived before he left, they would have hundreds of apartments to search. Still, he didn't want to risk that because it would make leaving tricky.

All of this was assumption on his part, but assumptions kept him from getting caught. For all he knew, there was merely an accident that the police were rushing to, but they weren't. In actuality, the police were searching for him; however, they were searching in an area he'd never been, thanks to one misdirection he'd let slip to make the job of finding him more difficult, just as imparting a false name to his victims. He knew that it would only be a matter of time before the police connected him to All Saints' Episcopal Church and that the priest would know who he was, so he'd called the priest one evening, pretending to be drunk, and let slip his location. He never knew whether the seed would sprout, and the information would be passed on to the police, but he left nothing to chance.

An hour later, he concluded the living room to be as footprint free as was possible. He then went to the bathroom to retrieve the trash, which contained the empty contents of his recent purchase of hair dye and nothing more. He tied up the bag and returned to the living room, placing the bag into a larger trash bag that sat next to his computer supplies.

Finally, he went into the bedroom to check on Consuela, sleeping on the bed. He carefully removed the IV that kept her sustained with fluids, nutrition, and sedatives, rolling up the IV line and setting it aside, then went to the bathroom and disposed of the remaining fluid in the IV bag. Once all of that was packed away in its case, he carried it to the front door, then returned and removed the adult diaper. He'd changed her a couple of times a day, so had a bag full of dirty diapers sitting beside the bed. He stuffed this last one in, sealed it tight, and then retrieved a pair of XL panties from a nearby drawer and slid them on her.

Once he was assured that her bedroom was as spotless and evidence-free as the living room, he enacted one final measure of safety, for himself. He pulled out a syringe of his personally prepared cocktail of Rohypnol/Melatonin from his satchel and returned to the bedroom. He could just use the Rohypnol, but he wanted to ensure they slept a long time; did not waken until he was far away. He lifted her fleshy arm, and slid the tip into a vein, depressing the contents into her blood stream.

"There now, you'll sleep for about eight more hours and then you'll awaken from your long, three-day nap with absolutely no recollection that anyone was ever here. And other than losing a few pounds and a bruise on your arm, you won't even realize you missed that time. Thank you for the loan of your apartment and your food stores. I am sorry that I interrupted your vacation. Perhaps you'll be able to do Jamaica next year. I wish I could replace the money you lost on the airfare, but that's the price paid for assisting me."

He recalled his encounter with Consuela three days earlier at his self-defense class. Consuela was one of those women who were so eager to be friends, or in a relationship with anyone that she tended to reveal far more about herself than was prudent. For Consuela, she was beginning her vacation to Jamaica the following day and looked forward to going home after class to pack for her flight, which was scheduled to depart at 6:30 the following morning. Perfect, in Christian's estimation. That meant that she wouldn't be missed at work, or by anyone else, for a good long while. He'd engaged her in conversation to ensure that the intended vacation would be alone, which it was, of course. Consuela was a lovely woman, in personality, but her outward countenance was less than appealing. This leant an air of desperation for finding a mate, which suited Christian's needs beautifully.

He'd talked her into dinner that evening, under the guise of starting her vacation off on a celebratory note, and ensured she knew it was his gentlemanly duty to see her home to her door, safely. From there, gaining entrance had been as easy as a kiss on the cheek, which he did again now prior to leaving her bedroom.

He gave the apartment a final glance and then opened the door into the hallway. He heard the sirens. They seemed closer. He always tried hard not to allow his brain to run amok with worries, but the sound of so many sirens caused him to wonder whether he'd exit the building and be surrounded by cops. He listened more intently and began to calm, feeling confident that they weren't at this complex yet. He sucked in a deep breath and peered into the hallway, as always ensuring that it was clear of people before heading out. A person might not give him a second glance if he were just wandering about the halls, but a neighbor might find it very suspicious if he were to exit from an apartment of someone known to him or her. He hadn't avoided capture by being stupid.

He quickly retrieved his gear and casually headed down the steps of the Kingsboro Place Apartments to stow it into the trunk of his car. During that time, he made a cursory glance about but did not yet see any uniformed officers. He felt his pulse slow, and relief flood his system. Still, it would be careless to linger, so he dashed up the steps and, after ensuring the coast was still clear, grabbed the trash bags and sprinted back to his car. He threw the bags in the back seat and would dispose of them in a dumpster on his way out. He sighed heavily in relief, turning over the ignition. A quick glance at his watch told him that he didn't have exceedingly long to set up for his next victim, find another apartment to borrow, and to locate another participant in his on-going experiments. That aggravated him, since what he really wanted was to head for the Georgia border.

The first couple of abductions in a new city were the easiest to pull off because he spent several weeks setting up for them. In this instance, he'd joined a local church and then started a martial arts class for women's self-defense at that church. He'd managed to abscond with two women using that cover. He'd also found a suitable apartment to use through that class from which to monitor Brooke Madison. And from the church's congregation, he'd found an apartment from which to monitor Sandra McIntyre. It belonged to a lonely old lady who admitted to spending her days watching television. He'd offered to stop by to visit with her, which she'd readily agreed to as "no one ever stops by to visit anymore." Perfect patsy, perfect location. They always were.

But perfect never lasted after the first two abductions. Police collected too much evidence, lost memories had victims seeking out police in filling in the gaps of their missing days; and even more chilling to him was the net that started closing in. That fear of capture always had him wondering why he just didn't quit—whether the police departments failed or not. Just allow the message to be given and hope they changed their ways. Less likely to be caught that way.

Every time he told himself that, he'd get angry again at their incompetence. He ran those tests, he reminded himself, to improve police response time. If he gave up, what message would that send? That they could stop caring about their citizens.

Fortunately, those police precincts who found victim number two in time were more in number than those with which a third experiment was required. If it got to a third victim, he would all but spoon-feed the police clues to ensure the victim *was* found. He never went beyond three abductions, because the longer he stayed in a city, the more likely it was the police, or a concerned citizen, would spot him. If he were arrested, he couldn't continue his experiments in other cities, so he rationalized that three was the maximum number of deaths with which to drive home the point that the police couldn't take their times locating a person gone missing. Still, to feel justified in quitting after the third abduction, he generally made it more difficult, by cutting the time allotted from thirty-six hours to half that time...or less.

"I won't be taking any risks after this city," he concluded. "I'm planning for all three abductions at the onset. Make things less frantic and anxiety ridden. Now though, first things first," he said to himself after dropping the bags in the dumpster at the head of the complex, "I need to find a way around all of those sirens."

He punched Hartsfield-Jackson Atlanta International Airport into his GPS and selected what he deemed the safest route out of that area. He didn't really need to go to the airport, but he knew that the police wouldn't be searching that region for him—yet. Once at the airport, he could start planning the abduction. He took the off-ramp towards I-85 southbound, then flipped on the radio and immediately perked up at the news broadcast.

Sources at the APD have confirmed that the perpetrator, known only as Christian Price, may also be responsible for at least twenty deaths in major cities all along the east coast.

Christian laughed without humor, "Well, I'm impressed. I thought you were intelligent when I spoke to you, but then you royally screwed up the search for Brooke Madison. Now, you've proven adept at finding out information. Still, if you're so smart, Detective Hardwick, how could you fail so miserably?"

His monologue ended when he spotted a sign for Grant Park, which made him mentally alter his route. He veered onto the off-ramp to I-20 E and then swung onto Boulevard toward the park. He never knew why he chose a particular community for his work, but he did know he'd have a better chance of finding his next victim in a neighborhood than at a bustling airport.

He spotted the Park Avenue Baptist Church, and grinned enthusiastically, pulling into the nearly over-flowing parking lot.

He glanced at his watch again. It was nearing 7 p.m., which meant that mid-week church services would be just beginning. There was always a single female among the churchgoers; always someone alone who proved an easy target.

He sat back and watched those entering the church. It wasn't long before he spotted a perfect pawn. She'd either be the one he'd be staying with or the one partici-pating in his experiment. He'd decide that later, but the thought had his mind drifting to his next experiment. An impish grin appeared on his face when he settled on a particularly malevolent trial, he'd conducted in Boston a while back. Particularly malevolent, because, unlike the gas he'd used several times now, this method of extinc-tion allowed for zero tardiness in police arrival. With the gassing method, the victim stood a chance at survival *if* the police arrived early or in the nick of time. Not a huge chance; and their life might prove difficult from that point forward, if they suffered ill side effects; but they'd still be alive.

He tended to reserve the method that allowed for zero tardiness for his third attempt; because by then, he was all but giving the police an address in which to find the victim. By the third try, the police should not fail. If they did…well, there was simply no quarter given. That last thought had him dialing the police precinct again.

Atlanta Police Department. Zone 5. Please hold.

"You've got to be kidding me," Christian snapped as he listened to the silence extend into minutes on the other end of the line. He nearly ended the call when it was reconnected.

Atlanta Police Department, Zone 5. How may I direct your call?

"I need to speak with Detective Hardwick. Urgently. It's regarding the kidnapping cases."

Please hold.

Christian grinned as he imagined Hardwick rushing to take his call; trying to calm himself before picking up the line.

This is Detective Hardwick.

"Detective, this is Christian Price."

Why don't you just dispense with the theatrics and tell me your real name?

"I didn't call to engage in banter, Detective. I called to tell you how angrily disappointed I am that you shifted your focus to finding me. It's the girls you should be concerned about, first and foremost."

You heard the sirens. Hardwick stated flatly, and Christian knew he'd been right that they'd been searching for him.

"I did, and I knew that you'd lost focus," Christian retorted.

Brooke was already dead. I need to find you before you take another woman hostage; before you kill again.

"Don't ever make me your focus again, Detective, or I won't leave Atlanta after this next abduction. Do I make myself clear?"

Hardwick went quiet, and for a moment Christian thought the line had gone dead—if not for the heavy breathing on the other end.

It's my job to stop you by any means necessary, Hardwick replied softly, his tone deadly. *Just because you don't happen to want to get caught doesn't mean that I'll stop looking for you. If I get to you, you don't get to claim any more lives.*

"Do you know why I left the other cities, Detective?"

I thought you weren't interested in engaging in banter, Price.

Christian laughed shortly, "I'm not, but I do feel the need to enlighten you. I left because the police officers, with whom I dealt, did what I told them to do. They found the girls. No more, no less."

After you wrapped up clues in a nice box with a bow on top, from what I understand.

"I told you that I don't really like killing, Detective, so I finally lend a hand the best I can without getting ensnared. It's not my intention to ever get caught, because if I do, my experiments will end and there are simply too many more police officers who need a jump start in their enthusiasm to catch criminals. The police have become too unconcerned. If I put police officers on alert, across the nation, that they must meet certain expectations, then perhaps less people will die. Maybe, just maybe, crime will go down, or more criminals will pay the price for their actions."

I will continue to hunt you down, Price, and eventually, I will find you.

"Well, then, I'd best let you know that I've left your district already—temporarily. Knowing that, I urge you to let the APD rest for now, because when I return to your district tomorrow evening, another woman's life will be on the clock."

Christian looked up and noticed the throng of people milling about outside had gone in and the sound of an opening hymnal reached his ears. He quickly hung up the phone and slid from his vehicle.

He needed to head inside to locate that petite African American woman he'd spotted. He didn't want to lose sight of her but lose sight of her he had. He quietly entered the church and peered in through the sanctuary doors to give the congregation a cursory glance and then turned and walked out. Normally, he would stay, find his quarry to see if she'd met up with someone inside; but this time he knew it wouldn't be prudent as he was the only Caucasian in the building. That would make him more memorable and memorable didn't serve him well.

He returned to his vehicle to wait for services to let out, hoping that the early autumn nightfall didn't prohibit him from spotting his target again. It didn't. At 9:15, she exited and immediately split off from the crowd, headed toward a gray Buick LeSabre. Apparently, though she attended church, she wasn't one of those who socialized with the members of the congregation. At least not on a mid-week evening service. That served his needs perfectly.

He started his engine and waited patiently for her to leave the parking lot. Apparently, she wasn't in a hurry, for he saw her silhouette from a streetlight, pick up a cell. That turned into a lengthy conversation.

Nearly every car in the lot was gone, which made him a bit jittery. If it came down to just her and him sitting there, she'd likely get suspicious. He nearly abandoned this person in search of another when he saw her lower the phone. A moment later, her engine roared to life and a smile lit his features. He'd left his car idling during her extended chat, so all he needed to do was shift into gear and follow her. He kept his fingers crossed, literally, as he steered through the winding streets around Grants Park, that this woman lived alone and that he'd be able to gain access to her without interference. A glance at his watch told him that he would have precious little time to locate another woman if this one turned out to be inaccessible. As it was, once he determined her role, he'd still need to find someone else to stay with and set up the experiment. He clenched his teeth—he hated rushed deadlines. Perhaps he should call the local media and change the tomorrow evening deadline given. Perhaps he would if the time crunch proved undoable. For a split second, he'd considered using this same woman as the victim and using her house as his headquarters. He dismissed the thought as fast as it entered his mind, because the home of a victim was almost always one of the first places investigators searched during and after a person was abducted. It was too great a risk. Another thought shot through his mind, but he dismissed it equally fast—rent a motel room for his operations. It would save time, to be sure, but he never did that, because he couldn't control that environment as he could the single owner of an apartment. Motel rooms meant using identification. There were also too many people to provide an identity should someone offer up a sketch to police or the media, as they had done here. No, better one person's memory to deal with than working with a bunch of unknowns.

He relaxed his jaw when she pulled into the drive of a small house, tall poplars bordered the property on both sides and a tall box hedge at the front of the property offered added seclusion. Moreover, she continued down the drive until she stopped at a gate to the rear.

"Oh, brilliant! This couldn't be more perfect," he purred, pulling to a stop along the heavily tree-lined sidewalk. The fact that it was perfect gave him reason to believe that his mission in life was just; that the fates wanted him to succeed in teaching the police a lesson. Otherwise, the police would have stopped him by now. A quick reflection on his prior abductions convinced him further that fate was on his side, because he'd snatched each woman as easily as he would this one. He had, in all abductions, played out the scenario as if scripted by providence.

He smiled and waited with God-like patience as she stepped back into her Buick and drove around to the back of the house before pulling into the driveway himself.

His timing had to be just as perfect now.

He knew he'd not be seen by anyone, because this property was designed for privacy. His grinned widened, but immediately faded, because he couldn't allow for cockiness. Just because the scene was perfectly set, didn't mean he could proceed haphazardly. Being cautious was why the police never caught him.

All he had to do was get through to the backyard before she finished parking and returned to shut, and perhaps lock, the gate; and hope she didn't get too alarmed when she saw him to raise an alarm before he managed to subdue her. He threw the car in park and quickly retrieved his supplies from the trunk, then climbed back in and slowly accelerated toward the back yard.

Luck remained with him as he maneuvered to park behind her sedan. She was still there, her head leaning back against the headrest. From his vantage in her rearview, he could see that she'd closed her eyes; and from the downed window, he could hear why. She was listening to what he could only surmise was a favorite song; and she didn't want to go inside until it finished playing. He wanted to laugh at how easy this abduction was going to go.

Cautiously, he collected his supplies and stepped from the car. Slowly, as to not alert her to his presence, he bent at the waist and tiptoed across the short expanse, grateful that there was grass beneath his shoes and not gravel.

He stopped by her window, and stared at her face, in

contented repose, and felt a momentary twinge of regret that it would be him that shattered her peace.

With swift reflex, his hand, holding a cloth saturated with chloroform, whipped into the window, and latched onto her face. He covered her nose and mouth securely, tightly, so to prevent the struggles and tugs of her hands from dislodging his.

Her eyes widened in fright. She stared at him, her gaze pleading for understanding; pleading with him to release her.

"I'm sorry," he whispered. "Hopefully, the police will find you and you'll continue with your life unharmed; with only a few nightmares by which to remember this moment."

Seconds later, her large brown eyes fluttered closed, and her body went limp. He waited a minute longer to ensure that her collapse wasn't a ruse. He wanted to make certain that the chloroform fully flooded her system so that he could prep the next step without fear of her waking up to scream.

When he was certain she was fully unconscious, he removed the cloth and shoved it into his coat pocket. From the other pocket, he removed a syringe containing his signature dose of Rohypnol and Melatonin.

He raised the woman's limp arm and located a vein on the inside of the elbow joint. He laid her arm on the top of the door and carefully slid in the needle. He'd done this so often, that he could nearly inject his mixture blindfolded.

Her body, already limp from the chloroform, deflated further before his eyes. She was now in as deep a sleep as was humanly possible and would remain that way well into the following day. He pulled open her door and slid his arms beneath her body, lifting her petite form with ease. When he reached his car, he laid her on the grass and then moved to pop the lid to his trunk.

Christian turned back and scooped her into his arms, depositing her into his trunk. He stood looking down at her for a moment longer, and then glanced at his watch. Since he decided she would serve as the victim for this next experiment, he now needed to find an ideal location to set up the perfect murder for the police to avert. After that, he'd need to locate someone willing to share their apartment for the next few days. It was going to be a busy night.

CHAPTER 17

As Christian made his way back to the nearly deserted streets of downtown Atlanta, his ire at Detective Hardwick's insistence on ignoring his dictates, elevated again. Hardwick hadn't allowed the APD time off to prepare, rather the streets appeared inundated with black and whites. The moment he spotted the first of the police vehicles, he veered off onto a side street and back toward the interstate.

"Why can't you be like the other police and do as instructed," he snapped. "There's a reason for those instructions, you know?"

In fact, the dictates given were often selfishly motivated. He didn't want the streets swamped with police because it made finding a suitable location more difficult. With police on high alert, he'd never be able to waltz unnoticed into an abandoned building with a body slung over his shoulder. Every other city department had heeded his advice and had sent the force home to rest in preparation of the coming challenge of locating the next victim.

He drew in a deep breath of irritation through his nostrils.

"Well, I didn't commit so many successful experiments by allowing the slightest hiccup in my plans to rattle me."

He drove about casually as any other Atlantian would; but his gaze was on high alert. It took him a while, but a thought came to him that had him laughing aloud.

"It would be almost too ingenious," he laughed, as he spotted the Bank of America Plaza a few blocks over from his current location. He took one-way street after one-way street—each time scanning the road as far as his sight could see to ensure it was clear, before turning onto it—until he finally managed to pull into the building's parking structure. He headed down to the recesses of the parking garage, knowing that many of the people who parked in these types of places always headed up; since most people were like trees—preferring to reach toward the sun, rather than wilt in the bowels of darkness.

He also knew, that while this place would be full of cars come tomorrow, the area that he needed for his experiment wouldn't likely be accessed until tomorrow evening; after his experiment was concluded. At least he hoped his supposition was correct.

As he made the final turn onto the lowest parking level, a quick glance about let him know that the structure was indeed deserted. From this point, it would only be a matter of time before his next experiment was set and ready to proceed.

He reached down and pulled the latch that would pop the trunk, and then stepped out of his car. It was important that his latest prey remain unconscious while he set everything up; otherwise, things would go to hell in a hand basket if she started screaming and banging on the trunk lid.

She remained immobile, limp, when he shoved at her shoulder, building his sense of security. He shut the trunk and returned to retrieve his pack from the back seat. His plans were intricate and took time to set up; but time wasn't always on his side.

CHAPTER 18

The news broadcaster never said when Price was going to make a return appearance. Do you think he's back yet?" Wilson asked, glancing at the clock on the wall. It read 6:30 p.m.

Hardwick too glanced at the clock, "His last call came at 7:30 in the evening. He told the media that it would be soon, so I'd say that it's a likelihood; still, I was kind of hoping that the police presence would deter him."

"Maybe it did, and he will call and say he's expecting a different district to handle this particular abduction."

Hardwick shook his head, "Doubtful. He needs us to prove we can do our job before he moves on, remember? It doesn't matter that our district is part of a whole, he selected us and therefore we're the target of his experiment."

"I know I'm a fairly new detective, but I can't see how we're going to do any better this time. We did everything humanly possible to find Brooke Madison. What can we possibly do different?"

"Despite our combined experience, our focus kept shifting to Price, where the clues led. Deep down, I think we kept assuming that if we followed the clues and found him that this would all end."

"Yeah, and normally that is precisely how it gets done, but we didn't start searching for Price until after... well, until the Madison case was closed."

"I know, but to answer your question, we don't follow the typical clues. We shove Price to the recesses of our brains and focus entirely on locating whomever he abducts next."

"But he doesn't give us very many clues in which to locate the victim..."

"He may this time. Remember his M.O?"

"Yeah, well, that may change because of the number of times you've pissed him off."

Hardwick grinned, but it held no humor. He realized that his partner was just agitated and was striking out at the only person nearby. It wasn't his fault that the women were abducted, and he certainly realized that it wasn't his fault that they weren't found in time; and it didn't matter if others thought to the contrary— including his partner.

"Sorry," Wilson muttered when Hardwick didn't respond to his accusation.

Hardwick didn't acknowledge the apology; instead, he called over the two detectives partnered with them, "Cortez, Harding."

"What's up?" Harding asked, rolling across the floor in his chair.

"It's nearing that time when we may be dealing with another abduction," Wilson supplied. "We think."

Cortez nodded solemnly, "So, what's the plan, Hardwick?"

"He'll call, and when he does, it's imperative that we listen carefully and do everything we can to find whomever he's taken next."

"I thought we did that automatically," Harding asked, his brow knitted in confusion.

"Yeah, it's all that we can do. If we do anything other than that, we'll lose another one," Hardwick snapped.

"I'm just hoping he's not too pissed at Hardwick to be stingy with his clues," Wilson stated antagonistic.

"I pissed him off. I got it, Wilson," Hardwick snapped more firmly, "so, drop it already."

"Yeah, Wilson," Cortez jumped in, "stop being a freakin' harpy, will ya? It's not like you're Mr. Infallible."

The three seasoned detectives looked at the rookie detective with expressions of irritability, which made Wilson purse his lips in a huff. "Fine, but I'm going to keep hoping he gives us more clues and more time."

"He'll give us more clues, but less time, as well you know," Harding supplied. "That's what he's always done when it comes to the third victim."

"I think a lack of sleep and success is making us all irritable..." Cortez started, but the phone rang, interrupting him.

Hardwick looked at the phone, raising his gaze to the clock. *If nothing else, he's punctual,* he thought.

He lifted the receiver and waited for the front desk sergeant to notify him of which line the caller was waiting.

Line 2 was all the sergeant stated, for he knew it was all Hardwick needed to hear. Hardwick punched the speaker button and then punched the blinking number *2*.

"Price?"

I see you were expecting my call. I could have done as before and simply had the victim call...

"Let's get to it, shall we? A woman's life is at stake. Last time you jumped the gun and Brooke Madison died," Hardwick stated, and every detective's eyebrow darted upward. This was the first any of them had heard of this theory. What Hardwick hadn't shared was the autopsy report, which he'd gone over just before 6 p.m.

I didn't... Price started, but Hardwick was in a foul mood and needed Price to realize that the police weren't the only ones who'd screwed up.

"Yes, you did. Brooke's death is on your head, not ours. We were well within range of her location at 7:30 a.m.; would have easily reached her and saved her life if you hadn't released the toxin early. That's right. I just got her autopsy report and it said she'd been exposed to a high concentration of venom for long enough to cause her to be dead before we arrived. We got there at 7:35 a.m. and when I broke into that room, the air was inundated with gas and those tanks were empty. According to your own actions, that gas shouldn't have released until precisely 7:30, if the door wasn't breached. We should have been able to get in there and get her out in time to save her life. Brooke didn't stand a chance. You either misjudged the amount of gas or you intended that she die. Either way, I'm letting the press know that Brooke's death is on your head. Now where is your latest victim or do you plan to deliberately kill her too?

Be careful, Detective. I've already decided that I don't like you.

That statement caused Wilson to glare at Hardwick,

but it went unnoticed by everyone except Cortez who glared back, daring Wilson, with his stare, to open his mouth and say something. Wilson chose to refocus on what Price was saying.

You have eighteen hours. I suggest you concentrate your efforts on parking structures. And detective, your time starts now!

The line went dead, and Hardwick immediately stood and started pacing.

"He's given us half the time to locate this one. Why?" Wilson asked.

"Think, Rookie; because he's told us where to concentrate our search," Harding supplied, watching Hardwick pace in agitation. "Why didn't you tell us about the autopsy report, Hardwick?"

Hardwick stopped packing, but before he could respond, the captain opened his door, "All of you, in here now," he barked and then returned his attention to the breaking news story in progress.

So, the race against time begins again. The anchor was saying as the four detectives filed into his office. *And the question on citizens' minds everywhere is, will they prove successful this time?*

The captain picked up the remote and turned off the set, then spun the chair to face his detectives, "Half the time."

Hardwick nodded.

"Does this guy even think before he acts?" The captain continued to rant, "Or does he not realize how many parking structures there are in the greater downtown area? Our entire cities infrastructure is reliant upon parking structures."

"We already have men on the streets, Captain," Hardwick interrupted. "We have better odds in locating the victim this time, since we know where to concentrate our efforts."

"And with it being nighttime, a majority of the parking structures will be vacant, right?" Wilson asked, "So we'll be able to spot a vehicle…" he stopped speaking when he noticed the looks beings sent his direction. "What?"

"There are also residential parking structures to consider, Wilson," Cortez stated, "which means hundreds of parked cars to search."

"No," Hardwick supplied, suddenly thoughtful. "She won't be in a car."

The captain shook his head and rubbed his eyes, then sighed, "What makes you jump to that conclusion?"

"Because of what Cortez just said," Hardwick said and then elaborated. "He wouldn't park a car with her in it in a busy parking garage, and then just walk away. There is too great a chance of a passerby spotting her;

and he doesn't want her found by a passerby. He wants the police to sweat out a search."

"So, then, we're back to him parking a car in a business garage; mostly deserted in the evenings?"

"But it wouldn't be deserted tomorrow, and we have until 1:30 tomorrow afternoon to locate her. So, same issue."

"So, then what? It's a ruse? A trick to throw us off..." Harding started.

"No," Hardwick interrupted. "He gave us credible information. What he didn't tell us, and what he wants us to ascertain for ourselves, is that he's placed her somewhere within a parking structure that's not a car."

"*¡Madre de Dios!* A maintenance closet!" Cortez blurted suddenly.

Hardwick nodded, "A maintenance closet sounds plausible."

"Okay, so let's say you've figured that much out," Wilson interjected, "that still leaves more garages to search than we potentially have the manpower for. And, if she's in a maintenance closet, wouldn't she draw attention if she started causing a ruckus? Anyone parking would hear her banging on a door just as they would if she were in a car."

"Good point," Harding muttered. "Nice call, Wilson."

Everyone remained thoughtful for a moment and

then Hardwick spoke up, "Suppose she's bound. She wouldn't be able to draw attention. In a car, bound or not, she could still bang on the car with her feet because the space is confined. So, I think our best bet is still maintenance closets; unless someone can think of some-place different?"

Everyone nodded in unison.

"Ok, so we're back to parking structures and mainte-nance closets."

"And," Harding interjected, "with as many as there are, we may easily overlook one. Do we even know where all of the parking garages are located?"

"It would be nice if there was a map denoting the location..." Cortez started, but was interrupted by the captain.

"Actually, I have an app for that."

"What?" Hardwick asked, stunned.

"Well, it won't show every single parking structure in the Atlanta area, but it will help us in not overlooking some that we may not think of readily." He passed over his phone, "Click on ParkWhiz."

Harding opened the app and scrolled through. "There are at least twenty here that we can search," he stated, astonished. "And we know that most corporate buildings have their own parking structures, and some residential buildings have their own. I'll be damned, we may just beat this thing. Captain, could you write down these locations and dispatch them to black and whites?

"Don't waste your time. I'll do a web search for parking structures," Cortez added. "This app may provide a good starting place, but I know for a damned fact that there are literally hundreds of places for parking in Atlanta."

"You compile a list, Cortez," Hardwick concurred. "As soon as you have it ready, get it out to all units."

"Wait," Wilson called, as the meeting appeared to be breaking up, "how do we keep from wasting our time by doing overlapping searches? I mean, if every black and white has a map, then..."

"Shit, they could waste time searching the same locations, which means someplace might get missed altogether," the captain concluded. "Yet another good catch, Wilson. You'll make a good detective yet. So then, how do we prevent overlap?"

"We do what we did when searching the warehouses. We create a completed search grid reference. This is going to be just as time consuming too. Captain, I think we need to call every black and white in off the streets now," Hardwick said, rubbing his face in agitation.

"Wilson, get word to dispatch to call in every available unit then go wake those who had off-duty rest time," the captain stated, and Wilson jumped up and left the office hurriedly.

"Captain, while we're waiting on the units to arrive, I think you need to get in touch with Channel 5 and every other news affiliate in Atlanta. It's time we deflate Christian Price's ego and reestablish not only a bit of faith in the Atlanta PD, but also restore some confidence in our own abilities. The people of Atlanta need to know they can rely on us; and our exhausted police force needs to know that there really wasn't any way to save Brooke Madison."

"What's on your mind?"

"Christian Price blundered his experiment with Brooke Madison, and the city needs to know it."

CHAPTER 19

O kay, everyone, quiet down," the captain stated to the room full of officers; the entirety of the Atlanta Police Department's Zone 5. "As you are all aware, we have less than sixteen hours remaining in which to locate the latest victim of the man we call Christian Price. To use that time effectively, we've broken down each sector into grids. I'll assign each group a grid to search, and search thoroughly. You don't want to overlook a building in your grid only to discover it was that building in which our vic was being held. Be vigilant. None of us wants the blood of this woman on our conscious. Let's show this perp, and the citizens of Atlanta, that we know how to do our job and we know how to do it right."

The captain waited only a moment for the shouts to die down and then continued. "To keep it simple, there will be four squads to a grid. Each car will be supplied a list of potential places to check within that grid. Keep track. Call in each location to dispatch and they'll mark it off on our primary map, along with the search time. When you hear a call over the radio from your search group, mark off the location they relay. You'll likely run across places that aren't on your map. Call it off to your group for them to denote so that they don't search it again. The key here is efficiency. We have limited manpower and limited time. Understood? Good. Now, we're going to call you up by car number. As soon as all four groups are assembled and provided lists, get moving."

"And remember," Hardwick interjected, "that we're focusing on maintenance closets within parking structures."

"Right," the captain concurred and then set about calling car numbers. It took another hour to dispense the lists to all the units and another half hour after that for everyone to get their cars out of the parking lot. "I only hope the search goes more efficiently than this, or we're in a world of hurt," he muttered to Hardwick as they watched the remaining black and whites pull out of the garage.

Hardwick shook his head, "We're down to fourteen hours left, and I have to admit, Captain, that I'm more than a little concerned. Price may think he's done us a favor, but he's obviously unfamiliar with Atlanta. Harding was right; there are literally hundreds of parking structures, and several maintenance closets in each one. How are we ever going to stop this man if we don't have the resources to do proper searches?"

"It's a concern I bring up at every budget meeting," the captain sighed heavily, "and a concern that gets shot down every time. There isn't any way to convince the pencil pushers of our need because they aren't out there on the front lines to see the damage their budgetary restrictions cause. And that's not a discussion for now; not when there's a woman's life at stake. I need you out there…"

"Doing what? We have black and whites searching every possible location. Wilson and I would just be the ones overlapping their searches. It's better if we stay here to…I don't know…to coordinate their efforts."

"I thought that was my job," the captain quipped humorlessly. "You need to be out there, coordinating in the field; listening to radio transmissions to ensure no building is left unsearched. That's what your team is expecting anyway," the captain concluded, nodding toward the other three detectives assigned to this case, sitting in a corner, waiting on Hardwick.

"Very well, Captain," Hardwick muttered, started down the steps, and then turned to the captain again, "I have to say though that I'm mad as hell at being manipulated like this, so when we do finally catch Price, I'm going to want a few minutes alone with him."

The captain chewed on his lower lip thoughtfully for a minute then nodded briefly. With a loud sigh, Hardwick turned and left the building.

CHAPTER 20

Sequoia knew her eyes were open, but she couldn't make out anything at all. It was dark as pitch and that made her nerves jumpy. As soon as her brain registered that, it moved to the next observation—she couldn't move. She was bound, hand and foot—and waist—to a chair. An awfully hard chair. Next for her brain to ascertain was that she couldn't speak. She poked her tongue out as far as was possible and closed her eyes in growing despair. Her mouth was covered with duct tape.

She tried to remain calm as the horridness of her circumstances flooded into her brain at once, but that attempt was completely shattered when her arm twitched, and she felt something pinch her skin.

Although she knew she wouldn't be able to see what it was; it was instinctive to try. Still, she didn't need to see it to know there was a needle in her arm, and the pinch of tape easily revealed there was a peripheral venous catheter attached. She was a nurse, so her brain formulated quickly that having a needle in the arm meant that there was something to be injected into her body—or extracted; however, since she couldn't feel the coolness of a liquid slithering through her veins, she could only draw speculative conclusions. The unknowing was unnerving.

She was about to start squealing to try to draw attention, when the door opened, flooding the blackened room with fluorescent lighting. The light was dim, but after being in complete darkness, it was startling enough to make her wince. Recognition dawned as her abductor stepped in, and she did start squealing. She fought against the restraints but was so securely fastened that her struggles didn't even budge the chair. She stopped struggling and stared at the man, wide-eyed, her breathing ragged.

"Okay, now that you've gotten that out of your system, we'll proceed. I can't stay long," he said, drawing a syringe from his jacket pocket, "since the search for you is well underway. I've given the police a particularly good clue as to your location, so you should make it out of here alive. However, I can't have you cheating by making too much noise. It's up to them to find you, not up to you to reveal your location."

The sight of the needle made Sequoia nauseous, but it also triggered something in her mind—that she had a needle in her arm, and with the light flooding the room, she could inspect that needle. Was the purpose of the peripheral venous catheter for him merely to inject a sedative into her body? The thought brought a small bit of relief to her worried mind.

Instinctively, she turned to inspect that intravenous catheter, following it upward to a medical bag…

She gasped behind the duct tape. It was full of an unidentifiable cloudy fluid and the knob meant to regulate administration was attached to…

She gasped again, as she felt a needle slide into the vein on her other forearm. She turned her head and watched with rising panic as her captor depressed the liquid from the vial. Slowly the contents emptied. The panic dwindled and she felt her head begin to swim; her eyelids grow heavier.

"There now," he whispered, bending to plant a kiss on her cheek, "you get some sleep. I gave you a higher dosage this time because I can't have you waking before the search is up…" he glanced at his watch, "in approximately twelve hours. You should waken before the deadline though, because I passionately believe that people should be lucid at the end of their lives."

He set to work, but despite the woman now being unconscious, he continued with his explanatory monologue. "If the police don't arrive before this timer reaches zero, it will trigger a series of events," he stopped talking long enough to check the wiring, wrapped around the dispensing knob, to ensure it was tight enough to turn fully when the mechanism was set into motion. He nodded in satisfaction and then finished his thought, "that will end with a massive dose of deadly venom from the Puff Adder rapidly flooding your system. Just a single injection from a Puff Adder bite may result in the loss of a limb, and if left untreated can kill a full-grown human within thirty minutes. Imagine then what the results will be from injecting the equivalent of ten bites. Pray they get to you first, for you don't want to suffer this fate."

He stiffened suddenly when he heard an approaching vehicle. Another glance at his watch showed it to be just after 1:30 a.m., which seemed far too early for someone to be arriving for work. He stiffened as the thought struck him that it could be a police officer making the rounds of this parking structure. A glance at his car, parked in the shadows, determined it was a fair sprint away; however, he'd not likely make it before the driver spotted him.

Still, he needed to distance himself from the victim. He shut the door and then darted over to a nearby concrete barrier, cursing that he'd left his equipment in the closet. He peered over the top but couldn't see any cars approaching. He cocked his head and listened carefully, judging the vehicle to be at least one level above. That meant he had time. Limited time, but better than no time at all.

He darted back to the closet and slipped inside; quickly collecting his remaining supplies. When done, he peered outside and when he still didn't spot the vehicle, he slipped out, maneuvering along the wall into the darkest recesses. He was halfway to his car, slithering from shadow to shadow, when a utility vehicle rounded the corner.

"Damn," he whispered, knowing that he'd misjudged the maintenance staffs' schedule. He'd assumed that no one would access the closets during nighttime hours; that the maintenance staff worked first or second shift; that everyone would have clocked out prior to this time of morning. He'd been wrong; and now there would be a price to pay.

"Damn," he muttered again when the vehicle pulled to a stop in front of the closet. He was unprepared for this unforeseen occurrence, which meant he'd have to think on his feet; something he wasn't very adept at, since he always planned everything carefully.

This also meant that he'd have to confront the worker; and if that worker proved young and fit...he inhaled sharply. He wasn't unfit himself; couldn't be in his chosen profession, but he was more on the slight build than the beefy build, which is why he never abducted men. Even slender men could hide a deceptively wiry strength; and he simply couldn't risk getting assaulted and injured; when he had so much work to do.

He suddenly started praying that the worker be old and infirmed; deciding that were providence indeed on his side in his experiments, then surely it would assist in ensuring they be successfully executed.

Executed.

The word popped into his head, and he knew what he had to do, but he only had seconds to prepare to do it. He quickly, quietly, rummaged through his remaining materials and grinned when he found something useful. He turned back, expecting to see the worker approaching, but he remained in his car, talking on his cell phone.

"Ah, if only people realized how distracting a cell phone could be," he whispered gleefully. Slowly, he maneuvered around the side of the concrete beam, and then crouched down and scooted quickly alongside of the utility vehicle. He stopped by the passenger side door when he heard talking and then realized that the man was still conversing.

"Yes, dear, I promise I won't forget," he was saying, "but shoot me a text just to be sure?" He laughed at her response, "Okay, I'll see you when I get home. Do try to get some sleep. Love you."

Christian pursed his lips and shook his head, *if you hadn't come into work, perhaps you'd have seen your woman later*, he thought to himself as he shimmied around to the front of the cart-like vehicle, remaining very low. When he reached the front bumper, he peered around the side, waiting patiently, like a predator after its prey. He knew he'd have to strike fast, and that his attack would need to be accurate, or he'd find himself in a likely unwinnable fight.

The door opened then closed and Christian's nerves jumped to high alert. He peered around the side one more time and sized up the maintenance worker as quickly as possible. It wasn't difficult. The man was short in stature—just slightly shorter than himself—and very slender. He sighed inwardly with relief.

With quiet tenacity, he quickly moved up behind the worker and threw the remnants of the catheter tube over his head, latching it onto his neck with determined vigor. With a grunt of effort, he tightened his grip, pulling firmly, until he heard the struggling man's breath begin to take on a gurgling sound.

To his credit, he struggled viciously, but he was no match for Christian's resolve; and his struggle was waning rapidly.

"Nothing personal," Christian said, as the man began to collapse, his breathing shallower. "You just came to work at the wrong time."

Without releasing his grip, Christian began tugging on the man, pulling him along like a heavy burlap sack, with nothing more than string as the handle. The distance to the concrete wall on the other side of the garage was about twelve feet away but pulling the man across the flooring using only the catheter was cramping Christian's fingers. He stopped pulling and dropped the body, "You have to be dead by now, right?" He asked, leaning down to listen for any signs of life. He heard none, so decided that it was safe to continue along, pulling the man by his feet. He covered the remaining distance quickly, then tugged and pulled until the man toppled over the concrete barrier into the overgrown grass below. He took a deep breath and then pocketed the catheter tubing, swiping his hands together, pleased with his work.

He looked back at the utility vehicle and tried to decide what to do with it, when another idea struck him.

He'd leave it right where it was. The placement of the utility vehicle would prove another hurdle for the police. Would they see it and assume that a maintenance worker already accessed the closet, meaning the woman couldn't possibly be there? Or would they utilize their limited brain power and decide to search the closet anyway?

He grinned, "This will indeed make for a good experiment." He turned back to the area in which he'd dumped the dead maintenance worker, "You've inadvertently done me a favor, too bad I couldn't return it and let you live. Time to find a place to set up my equipment so I can keep a sharp eye on things."

Christian climbed into his vehicle but stopped short of pulling onto the main street when he spotted two police cars a few blocks away. He put his car into reverse and turned around, heading up to the top of the parking structure. He wished he hadn't set the start of this experiment so close to the close of the last, it left him precious little time to plan appropriately, and he hadn't found a suitable place in which to set up his gear. That meant his only recourse was to stay put and monitor from his car. He sincerely doubted that the police would be searching vehicles for his latest victim. At least he hoped not. Perhaps he should call and amend his clue to specifically search... no, too easy and they'd never learn a thing.

He parked near two other vehicles, surprised there

was any cars there at all; grateful to know that there were those who burned the midnight oil like he did. He turned off his ignition and pulled out his laptop, connecting to the first unsecure Wi-Fi signal he could snatch hold of. As soon as he procured a signal, he turned on the camera he'd set up in the closet. He knew he wouldn't be able to see anything in the darkness, but he would be able to see if anyone breached the door.

He turned up the volume, then lay his head against the headrest. He'd never had so much time to wait for something to transpire, not without having something to do while waiting. The sudden drop in activity lowered the adrenaline pumping through his body and weariness set in. His eyes drifted closed, and he fell asleep.

CHAPTER 21

B lack and whites are beginning to return from their assigned patrols..." the captain started but Hardwick interrupted him.

"And not one has located our victim? Shouldn't we have them start another search?" Hardwick asked, concern lacing his tone. He stared up at the map they'd placed in the dispatch office, noting all the marks that dotted the paper. There were so many that he knew doing a re-search would be futile. The captain verbalized his thoughts aloud.

"There's no time. We've only got thirty minutes..."

"Twenty-six minutes, to be precise," Wilson interjected. "Sorry." He added quickly before they could chastise him.

The front desk phone rang, interrupting the captain's retort. He reached over and snatched up the receiver before the front desk sergeant could.

"Go!" He snapped at the caller. He sighed heavily after replacing the receiver and his brow etched with deep concern as he turned back to his detectives, "The last of the patrols are headed back now. I've instructed all officers to reassemble for a final—and hopefully speedy—evaluation on what we may have overlooked."

"I don't get it," Cortez snapped. "We've covered every possible avenue. Dotted all our Is and crossed all our Ts, but we've still managed to screw up somewhere. Could he be playing us?"

"You mean did he feed us false information to get back at Hardwick?" Wilson asked. This time, despite the looks of disgruntlement, Wilson didn't apologize. Instead, he raised his chin a notch, "Don't tell me I'm the only one thinking it. Hardwick has been riding this guy since the Madison abduction, and Price made it clear that he didn't like you none," he concluded, turning to face his partner.

"I thought we already clarified that the information was legit. We all agreed it was legit, despite his animosity towards me. What I think, Wilson, is that you're over-looking the fact that he wanted us to find this one; he didn't want to have to move on to a fourth victim.

Because he knows that the more times he's forced to abduct someone, the greater the chances he'll screw up and get caught; and the last thing this guy wants is to get caught. So, no, I don't think he fed us misinformation; I think one of our patrols screwed up."

"Shit," the captain muttered. "That's a monumental assumption, Hardwick."

"Maybe," Hardwick defended, "but it's also the most logical one."

The captain sighed heavily, "Well, if that's the case, let's see if we have time to find out which patrol it was and pray we have time to right the wrong. Let's go."

The four men filed from the captain's office and entered the conference room where once again every member of the APD's Zone 5 converged. They stopped milling about, murmuring to one another when they saw their superiors enter. Each one quickly took a seat and waited for the captain to take his place at the podium.

"We have twenty minutes to find this girl," he said without preamble, "yet each member of my department has returned empty handed. Not a damned clue as to where she is. That means that we either overlooked a place or failed to check them all. Now, which is it and what can we do to rectify it?"

The members of the force started discussions among themselves, and with each passing minute, the knit in the captain's brow deepened. When the clock ticked down to nearly ten minutes remaining, he knew that their chance of saving this next victim was nearly nonexistent. He wanted to cry out of sheer frustration.

And then two of his patrolmen stood.

"Sir," one called out, "we think we know where she could be."

"Well, damn it, speak up!" The captain shouted.

"Tell me in the car," Hardwick amended, jumping from the stage, and running toward the two patrolmen. "With me!" He yelled, as he sprinted past.

They ran to the parking structure and nearly pulled the doors off the hinges of Hardwick's Crown Victoria in their haste to hit the road.

At the entrance of the parking garage, Hardwick snapped, "Where are we headed?"

"Bank of America Plaza," one of the officer's responded.

Hardwick's brow knitted, but he didn't question their response. He slammed his foot down on the accelerator at the same time that he flicked on his lights and sirens. Then picked up the radio and called it in, "Bank of America Plaza. Dispatch an ambulance and the hazmat unit too. Don't wait. We don't want a repeat of last time," he concluded and then turned his attention back to the officers. "Johnson. Peters. Why there?" Hardwick waited for their response, as they raced toward their destination; but neither officer seemed inclined to share. "Why there?" He repeated with more force. The two officers glanced at each other and then at the floorboard.

"There's a room we didn't check," Johnson responded quietly, his tone full of shame and remorse.

"Why not? What in heaven's name would possess you to ignore your orders..."

"There was a maintenance vehicle parked in front of it," Peters snapped in their defense, as if that justified everything.

"Someone better start explaining or I'm going to beat you both to a pulp," Hardwick snarled.

Peters sat up a bit straighter and explained what happened, "We were on patrol, doing as we'd been told," he defended. "When we reached the lower level of the Plaza's parking structure, we saw a maintenance car parked in front of that particular closet. Since the maintenance worker had already been in there, we reasoned that there was no way the victim could be in there. After all, wouldn't the guy have called the police if he'd found her?"

"So, if you're so certain you made the right call, why are we headed there now?"

Again, both heads bent and then Johnson spoke up,

"Because no one else seemed to have overlooked one of the closets in their grid."

"If they had, we wouldn't have needed to speak out about the one we overlooked, because we would have been more certain that we were right," Peters snapped belligerent.

"If she dies, I'll see that you are both kicked off the force," Hardwick retorted, and then started swearing up a blue streak when he saw the time. One minute remained.

He spun the car's wheel sharply, skidding along the pavement, and nearly collided with the side of the BoA Plaza building as he worked to right his trajectory. The car bounced sharply as they hit the first speed bump; but Hardwick wasn't slowing any more than was necessary to prevent his crashing into a concrete barrier.

"Damn it all to hell and back," he yelled as the seconds ticked down far quicker than his decent, "why did this garage have to have so many levels?"

With three levels to go, the radio squawked, "Detective Hardwick, we have a call to dispatch."

Hardwick yelled loudly in anger, but ignored the dispatcher, willing his car to move faster. He rounded the corner of the lower level and slammed on the brakes, sending his car skidding dangerously along the oily surface. Moments later, it rammed into the concrete barrier, jarring the men inside, but none wasted a moment releasing their seatbelts and jumping from the vehicle.

"Be alive. Be alive," Hardwick chanted to himself as he ran across the short expanse. In the back of his agonized mind, it registered that the utility vehicle that caused the officers to forgo their search remained parked where they'd spotted it earlier in the day. That meant that the APD would most likely be searching the area for another body; but he couldn't dwell on that right now.

He reached the door and yanked it open expecting acrid gas to assault him, but there wasn't any this time. He didn't know whether to be relieved or not.

"How long before the ambulance arrives?" It was a rhetorical question, because none of them really knew when to anticipate the arrival, and since neither officer knew, neither answered. Hardwick sized up the interior of the closet quickly and then his gaze fell on the woman in the chair. Her skin was already bloating, and she was barely breathing. He knew instinctively that Price had injected her with some form of toxin. If that observation were accurate, he knew there wasn't anything he could do for her; and neither would the paramedics be able to, if they weren't carrying anti-venom; and the right anti-venom at that. Still, he wasn't one to quit that easily.

Within a split second of making that observation, he spotted the half-full medical bag hanging above her head; and then the IV catheter protruding from her arm. He took a step, and quickly, carefully, pulled the needle out and then pulled a switchblade from his pocket.

"Grab the AED from my trunk," he called and began cutting the ties that bound the victim's hands, feet, and waist. When he finished, she fell forward into his embrace, completely limp—and lifeless—he observed in frustrated anger.

He lifted her and moved her from the closet, laying her down on the concrete flooring with care. He was pleased to see that the two officers had not only retrieved the AED with haste but had proceeded to prep and charge it. He breathed a sigh of relief that they wouldn't waste even more precious time; especially since she'd completely stopped breathing at this point. There was no way he could be certain that shocking her heart muscle would even help, but he felt powerless and needed to do something. If the paramedics were there, they'd have attached the paddles to Hardwick's chest and turned up the power all the way as retribution for his stupidity, for they knew, even if Hardwick didn't, that if he started the blood flow through her veins again, the venom would begin circulating much faster. Yes, she was officially deceased, but the less venom circulating, the less damage to vital organs—potentially.

Hardwick opened the victim's shirt and placed the paddles according to the instructions. He heard tires screeching and looked up, hoping that it would be the paramedics. It wasn't. The van that rounded the bend was from Channel 5; and, before it came to a full stop, Cassandra Bouchard leapt out, followed rapidly behind by her cameraman, who worked to get his camera rolling.

"Keep them away, or I'll kill 'em," he snarled at the officers, who quickly stood to form a two-man human barrier.

"You found the latest victim, but is she alive?" Cassandra called out as soon as she was certain they were live on air.

CHAPTER 22

Christian had awakened long before as he heard cars screeching through the parking structure. A glance at his watch told him that they'd again arrived too late; that the venom had been dispensed. Still, it was so close to the dispensed time that he held out a modicum of hope that she'd survive. He didn't want to kill again.

He turned on his computer to check the camera he'd placed in the closet. There was no change. Hadn't been since he first looked. All was still dark in the closet; still quiet.

He reached for his phone knowing that he needed to assist Hardwick at this point if the woman was to live. He may have been delayed in reaching her; but he had arrived nonetheless, so the least he could do, to acquit this city, was to help him one final time in saving the woman's life.

Atlanta Police Depart...

"Patch me through to Detective Hardwick," he interrupted. "Time is of the essence."

One moment please. I'll attempt to make that connection.

Precious minutes ticked by, and Price's agitation mounted. A couple of minutes later, the dispatcher returned.

I'm sorry, but I'm unable to reach Detective Hard...

Christian hurled the phone against the passenger door.

After sucking in several deep, calming breaths, he reached for his phone and dialed the local news affiliate, knowing that their reporter wouldn't be far from wherever the activity was. If he was to know whether the woman lived or not, he'd need eyes down there, now that Hardwick had arrived and pulled the woman out of the closet and out of his view.

As he waited for someone to pick up at the newsroom, he opened a new tab on his laptop and clicked the live news link. He immediately disconnected the call when he saw Bouchard on the screen, waving her cameraman toward the scene. He turned up the volume.

Cassandra Bouchard was attempting to elicit a response from Detective Hardwick –

"You found the latest victim, but is she alive?"

"Yes, Detective, do tell us, did you get to her in time? Is she alive? I'm curious if you can save her," Christian directed the question at the computer screen so didn't really expect a response. All he sincerely hoped for was to see signs of life.

Hardwick didn't reply to the questions being hurled at him. The detectives continued to step in front of the camera making it difficult to see what was happening, but they veered the wrong way once and the camera picked up a quick image of the struggle for life going on, on the cold concrete floor of the Bank of America Plaza parking structure.

Christian's gaze widened and he sucked in a slow breath as his gaze raked over the swollen flesh already putrefying.

"If you'd taken my call, I may have been able to prevent this loss," he murmured, rage burning his mind.

* * *

THE DETECTIVES CROWDED around the flat screen television seated atop the captain's desk; each man holding his breath as they watched the electricity surge through the body of Sequoia Richardson. Her body arched just seconds after Hardwick called "clear".

"I get that those officers are attempting to prevent the public getting a firsthand view of this atrocity, but I'm ready to knock their heads together, because *we* need to see what's happening," Harding snapped.

Just then the ambulance arrived. With simultaneous shouts of outrage, each officer stood, futilely attempting to peer over the top of the ambulance on the screen. None knew whether she would be transported to the hospital or the morgue, because not one could see now whether she was alive.

FROM HIS CAR atop the BoA Plaza parking structure, Christian too grew more agitated and attempted to see what was happening as the ambulance skid to a halt; a position that blocked the sporadic view of the Channel 5 camera. When Cassandra Bouchard attempted to relocate for a better vantage, the two officers, placed in charge of preventing her access, stepped in front of her and stopped her from changing her location.

The viewing audience has a right to know what's going on! Christian heard her declare loudly.

"That's right," he concurred. "We have a right to know what's happening, so move you imbeciles! Me especially! I need to know."

By the time he'd concluded that one demand, it was too late. The ambulance was on the move and so were the two police officers. They took off at a dead run toward their superior's battered vehicle, jumped inside, and sped off after the ambulance.

Christian watched, only mildly amused, as the newscaster and her cameraman also bolted for their van; the cameraman doing all he was capable of to keep his camera rolling—and steady.

Christian heard the sirens since he was right above the place from where they were leaving, but he would only be able to monitor the girl's progress through the news channel's coverage, and that coverage was now being prevented.

The camera feed was still rolling as the van reached the mouth of the parking structure only to have a blockade of police cars impede their pursuit.

He screamed at the computer screen and slammed the lid.

"You should have never ignored my call. If you hadn't...argh," he yelled. With alacrity, he reached for his disposable cell and dialed the precinct.

Atlanta Police...

"This is Christian Price. Get word to Detective Hardwick that he needs Puff Adder anti-venom, and you better pray to God that you got that the first time."

He then called the news station and reiterated the message to the receptionist in the same angry, clipped tone.

He hit the *disconnect call* button on the cell and threw it at the window again, knowing that if he continued hurling his cell, he was going to break it or the window of his automobile.

Christian sighed and lifted the computer screen, turning it back on. He hated that he'd been disconnected from the live feed—as had all viewers—but he needed to keep the connection up for when the reports started up again. He had to discover whether Hardwick got the news and whether the woman lived.

"Pray she lives, Detective Hardwick," he whispered, "or by God the next person I take will make you wish she did."

CHAPTER 23

The captain's phone beeped, and he picked up the receiver, still watching the drama unfold on his screen, as Cassandra Bouchard went toe-to-toe with his officers, then the news feed went black, and the coverage reverted to the two anchors.

Captain, the front desk officer said immediately, *Christian Price called in and said to get a message to Detective Hardwick. The doctor needs Puff Adder anti-venom.*

"Got it. Thanks."

The captain clicked the remote and shut off the television. He immediately picked up his cell and dialed Hardwick directly. It rang five times and went to voice mail. He hit *redial,* tapping his fingers on his desk while he waited. After three *redial* attempts, Hardwick finally answered.

What?

"Hardwick, this is the captain. If you made it to the hospital, tell the doctors that she needs…"

We're at the morgue.

"Shit."

Yeah, I've been saying that a lot since we crawled into the ambulance. So, what were you going to tell me?

"Price called. He said to relay a message to you that the girl needs—needed—Puff Adder anti-venom to save her life."

Son-of-a-bitch!

"You couldn't have known."

Yeah, I could've. If I had taken Price's call. Dispatch tried to put him through to me, but I didn't…Oh, God! If I had taken the call, I could've alerted the ambulance to have the anti-venom; I could've…Oh God. I killed her.

"Breathe, Hardwick. I think you're losing perspective here. The ambulance wouldn't have had it if you'd known because they were already en route. If you look at this rationally, which you aren't at present, Price killed her the minute he injected her; and, if I must keep perspective too, two of my officers probably leant a hand in her death by overlooking that closet—something I have to deal with

173

rather shortly. Anyway, by the time you got to her...I saw her body lying on the concrete; bloated and blackened as it was. She was already dead. Come back to the precinct. Let the coroners do their job. I need you here to do yours."

You know he's going to do this again. Hardwick's tone was flat, and he sounded beaten. The captain drew in a sharp breath as he imagined his best detective defeated by a madman, and for a moment he wanted to join in the detective's pity party. After all, if his best detectives couldn't stop this insane nut job then he couldn't imagine anyone who could.

"Yeah, he's going to do it again, and I need you here so that when that call comes in, we can..."

What can we do different, Captain? We did everything right this time...

"No, we didn't. Come in. We'll discuss what happened and discuss what to do about the two officers who royally screwed this investigation. Do you need a lift?"

No, Johnson and Peters followed the ambulance in my car. Shit! I'm gonna need a new car. Double shit! Captain, you need to have one of the units on scene stay there.

"Why, what gives?"

The missing maintenance worker. Something tells me that a search of the surrounding area is going to turn up another dead body.

"You think Price killed the maintenance worker and then parked his vehicle in front of the closet, just to throw us off the scent?"

No, I think it's more likely that the maintenance worker arrived for work at an inconvenient time, parked there, interrupted Price's work, and lost his life.

"Damn. Nothing worse than wrong place, wrong time. Okay, I'll have a black and white remain on site and do a search for this missing worker. You come on in."

CHAPTER 24

It was several hours later when the news broke about Sequoia Richardson's death.

Christian had been tapping his fingers on the wheel impatiently for the entire time, waiting expectantly as the news broadcasters filled the time prior to the announcement with a story of Sequoia's life—after they'd discovered her identity.

A viewer watching the news had recognized Sequoia's swollen face and called it in. From that point, the news was flooded with her life and accomplishments. They'd even dispatched a reporter to try to obtain an interview with family members but all they'd been able to report was that *"the family is too distraught at present to speak with anyone."*

It wasn't until the news anchors interrupted one of their reporters with "breaking news" that Christian relaxed the tapping, listening intently.

We've just received word that Sequoia Richardson was indeed pronounced dead during transport and was taken directly to the morgue, Patricia Wheaton stated, her expression saddened; but Christian knew that her affectation was a ruse. She was probably jumping for joy inside because bad news meant higher viewer ratings. He sighed as he continued listening to their exchange.

What do you think this means for the citizens of Atlanta? Charles Braxton asked, but his co-anchor didn't reply. It was as if the gravity of the situation sank in with the suddenness of a brick thrown into water and everyone realized that another Atlanta citizen was likely to be murdered—and soon.

"I'll tell you what it means," Christian answered the query in a treacherous tone, "it means that for the Atlanta Police Department to take me seriously, I'm going to have to hit closer to home. They're going to stop blaming me for their incompetence and start taking my calls."

CHAPTER 25

Solemn faces filled the captain's office an hour later. No one spoke for the longest time as each processed the results of yet another failure.

All four detectives sat around the room in deep contemplation, but the captain had officers Johnson and Peters remain standing at attention. He sat glaring at them and then finally felt confident enough to question first, not kill them both first.

"Tell me again what happened," he asked, keeping a tight rein on his calm demeanor.

Johnson and Peters glanced at each other, and then Johnson began to relay the details again, "When we arrived at Bank of America Plaza, we inspected all of the maintenance closets; but when we arrived at the lower level, there was a maintenance vehicle parked in front of the last closet. We made an erroneous assumption that the worker would've informed APD if he'd found a body. With time in short supply, we felt we'd be better served searching our other locations. We didn't know, until we returned to APD that we'd likely made an error in judgement."

"Explain to me why you thought you could make that sort of major decision without consulting a superior officer," the captain barked after the officers relayed, again, their version of events after seeing the utility vehicle, "especially when you knew the direness of the situation and were explicitly instructed not to overlook a single solitary closet. One radio call..." The captain closed his eyes and drew in several deep, calming breaths as he felt himself rapidly losing control of his temper.

"We assumed..." Peters started but was interrupted.

"Well, you assumed wrong, you jackasses," Cortez snapped.

"Easy Cortez," Hardwick interjected. "Precious time was lost because of the decision you two made. Had you not assumed; had you consulted with the captain, then there is no doubt that Sequoia Richardson would still be alive. I've checked your records. You called in the search of the Bank of America Plaza two hours before deadline. Two hours. That venom wasn't released into her system until Price's deadline was reached, so if you'd have checked the closet..." It was Hardwick's turn to stop talking and take deep breaths. If he had his way, he'd strangle these two officers; draw out their very life force, run to the morgue, and inject that into Richardson's lifeless body.

After several more minutes silence, the captain finally spoke up again, "Because of your blunder, a woman lost her life and Price, likely, is going to abduct someone else; so, someone else's life will likely now be on the line. Therefore, I'm recommending to IA that they forgo an investigation and terminate your employment with the Atlanta Police Department, posthaste. Based on the overwhelming evidence available and your own admission of incompetence, I see little need to drag things out with an investigation that will draw the same conclusions and result in the same outcome. You are, of course, entitled to seek council and are, of course, entitled to request an investigation despite my recommendations; however, be advised that if you try to change your stories or place blame at anyone's doorstep but your own, I will also recommend that you be charged with accessory to murder. You also know that this interview is being recorded, so any attempts to weasel your way out of this won't work. At this point, IA may very well turn you over to the DA for prosecution without even consulting me. You're both just fortunate that the press didn't get wind of your royal screw up because if anything causes them to shift focus away from the lunatic that we are trying to stop onto the ineptitude of the APD, I will end you myself. Now get out of here and clear out your desks. You're both suspended pending further notification. If I thought it was safe, I'd have you both out of this building before the shit hits the fan again; however, I can't risk someone seeing two members of the APD leaving to go home, so you're to stay in the building until this is over."

"When do you think that's likely to happen, precisely?" Wilson asked solemnly, as Johnson and Peters shuffled from the room. "The shit, I mean. Any word from Price?"

The captain shook his head, "No, we haven't heard a peep, which I'm certain, in this case, does not translate to good news."

CHAPTER 26

A few blocks from the precinct office, Price sat watching the activity of officers milling about the grounds: his gaze narrow, his breath fuming. He parked along the curb next to an adolescent oak, with branches just high and wide enough to cast his car into the shadows. His purpose for selecting this spot was simple—he needed a place that would obscure him from any traffic or building cameras that might be in the area.

Had he been thinking rationally at this point, he would simply abandon this city and chalk this experiment up to a disastrous failure. It was obvious after the Sequoia Richardson fiasco that this department was beyond hope and that made him feel a deep sorrow for its citizens.

The sorrow vanished and his ire elevated when he thought about how simple it should have been for the police to locate Richardson. He'd given them every opportunity to find her in time; had all but drawn a map with an "x" marks the spot. Still, he'd realized that the scene had been set for possible failure, with the arrival of the maintenance worker. He knew that a passing patrol could very well assume that the worker had accessed the closet already. Perhaps the failure had been his in crediting the officers with more reasoning skills than they possessed. He sighed heavily. It didn't matter, for they'd still botched her rescue.

He didn't know what he was going to do yet, but he knew that it would need to send a message that no officer at the APD would be able to overlook. First though, he needed to locate a place nearby to set up his equipment. Remaining in his car at the upper level of the parking structure had seemed a logical choice at the time, but the number of police officers coming and going had made him more nervous than he'd ever been prior. It had become an active crime scene, so he was incredibly surprised that he'd been able to leave without being waylaid by any number of police officers nearby. Apparently, they hadn't thought that the murderer would be casually leaving the scene of the crime, so no one attempted to stop or question him. As far as they knew, he was just another employee being asked to leave the area.

He certainly needed to leave this area. It wouldn't be long before someone noticed his vehicle, so he started up his engine and pulled onto Ted Turner Drive in search of the nearest apartment complex. He didn't have time to find the perfect patsy this time; there simply wasn't time. He needed a place to set up, lay low, and start planning.

No matter who he decided to abduct this next time, he was going to need days to plan now that he'd gone past his self-imposed safety time zone. To him, it was like starting over in a new city; and starting over required planning. The thought had his nerves skipping. He'd never remained in a city this long and never had to arrange so many abductions, which caused him to shiver nervously. If he didn't prepare carefully, he'd be on death row after this, and he couldn't allow that to happen.

"Think," he whispered, rapping on his head. "How can you make the APD really sorry for messing things up this time?" He continued to rap on his head as he pulled into an apartment complex's parking lot around the corner from the APD. He slowly drove in circles to ensure there was no activity around the building. No police presence or heavy pedestrian traffic. If he were going to find a place in this building, he'd need to come and go unseen.

When he was confident as he could be that he could find an apartment here without fear of detection, he parked in a far corner, climbed out of his vehicle, and approached the first apartment he came to on the lower landing. He knocked sharply and waited. There was no response.

"Possibly at work," he muttered. He looked about surreptitiously and leapt over the patio railing. He hoped that the current tenant felt secure enough or was careless enough to leave their patio door unlatched. He tugged at the door and grinned as it slid open. He couldn't believe his luck, and once more, attributed his good fortune to fate's intervention.

He walked in, trying to ascertain just how many people resided there. If a family, he'd have to move on to another apartment and prayed his luck held. Subduing one person was tricky enough. Subduing parents and children...he didn't want to risk it. His fortunate continued to hold as he moved about the place. It was a studio apartment, which meant either a single person or a couple. He made his way to the bathroom to see if he could clear up that question and was nearly giddy when he found only one electric toothbrush on the counter. His relief waned slightly when he also saw the men's razor next to it.

This left him with a choice to make—attempt to take

the resident by surprise when he arrived home or attempt to find another place to occupy. He paced the small studio and quickly came to a decision.

With a quick peak out the door, he made his way back to his vehicle and hauled everything back to the apartment. He didn't know what time to expect the arrival of the resident, but he had work to do in the meantime. When the resident arrived back, he'd just have to be ready for him.

He'd just set everything down when he heard a movement outside the door. He nearly jumped out of his skin, but quickly composed himself, rooting quickly in his satchel for the chloroform and cloth. As soon as he had both firmly in hand, he dashed to stand out of sight next to the front door. It was then his gaze fell on the lock. He'd not secured it again, which meant the apartment dweller may become suspicious...the doorknob turned.

As always, Price knew he'd need to act fast if he were to subdue his prey. He only prayed that the man entering wasn't over six feet or getting the chloroform over his nose was going to prove difficult.

The door swung open, and the shadow of the person filled the room. It was a big shadow.

Damn! Christian exclaimed tacitly and for the first time in a long time, he found himself having to think on his feet; to act without forethought.

Without hesitation, Christian lowered his stance and rammed into the door as hard as he could, knocking the person against the jamb. It was a sharp enough thud to daze the man, but not enough to knock him off his feet. Christian needed to move fast. He recovered his footing quickly and then moved swiftly around the door, kicking at the man's knees sharply. The man grunted and fell. Christian moved behind him and slapped the chloroform rag over the man's mouth. If the chloroform didn't work quickly though, or if he'd failed to apply sufficient liquid to the rag, he knew he'd be in for a world of hurt since this man was so muscular as to raise suspicions of steroid use.

Christian pressed the rag more firmly over the man's nose and mouth, as the man's arms started to flail slightly; however, it was too little effort too late. The chloroform began to do its job. As always though, he wasn't taking any chances that it was ruse, bending so he could keep the rag firmly in place. His nerves were on fire as he waited for what seemed an interminable amount of time. Not only was he at risk of this man not becoming fully unconscious, but also that someone else would come strolling along and witness the goings on.

When he was certain it was safe, he tugged at the man's arm until he cleared the portal and then shut the door. Muttering about inconveniences beneath his breath, Christian went back to his satchel and retrieved a syringe of his sleep formula. He always kept plenty on hand, in the event he needed to incapacitate someone efficiently and speedily—as now.

"Now to ensure you don't awaken from your nightmare anytime soon." Without hesitation, he grabbed his limp, bulky arm and jammed the needle into the vein. Under any other circumstance, when he wasn't so agitated, he would take his time, reassuring the person on the receiving end of his machinations, that they would be simply fine. He would coo and stroke; all to ease those nightmares that he assumed they'd have for years to come. He knew the Rohypnol would erase many of their memories, but memories didn't necessarily remain gone forever. He'd also, under optimal conditions, drag the occupant to their bedroom to position them cozily on their beds. That wasn't going to be possible in this circumstance because of the man's weight.

He knelt down next to his current detainee, sighed heavily and sighed again, "Just using you would make this far more efficient. I could simply call in that the next victim is at the Highland Walk Apartment Complex. The police would swarm into the area, lock it down, and find you in less than three hours. By the time they arrive, I could be in my car and headed on to the next city on my list. That would be the smartest move, since I'm running low on supplies and even lower on ideas, but what good would that do? That wouldn't require any detecting on their part. Of course, telling them where Sequoia Richardson was located didn't require any detecting either. Come to think about it, no detective work has ever really been required by the local police."

Daniel—better known to law enforcement as Christian Price—stood and started pacing, angry again.

"I'm not effecting any change at all, am I? The only detective work that's been done was when Hardwick was after *me*. In every other circumstance, the victims were only located because I fed the police clues as to their whereabouts. Just how is this making the police more efficient; less apathetic?"

Daniel started pounding on his head again, now trying to justify his taking of lives to improve local law enforcement procedures. "How can I make them truly accountable for the individual I seize, if all they have to do is follow a few crumbs to the location? I need to change that. I need to find a way to make them use what limited brainpower they seem to possess. Think, Daniel, think!" He began pounding on his head again as he paced about the room, like an unwilling fighting Pitbull in its captor's cage. When the pounding produced no more than a headache, he sat down, and started breathing in and out slowly through his nostrils, "Okay, let's review what transpired here: With Sandra McIntyre, I didn't offer the police any clues at all. The husband simply reported her missing; just as I did with my wife. After thirty-six hours, I placed an anonymous call to the police informing them that there was a body found in the warehouse district. That was the same length of time it took for someone to locate my wife's body and report it to the police.

"Up until I kidnapped Brooke Madison, the McIntyre case was still open; still ongoing. No clues, no apparent chance of solving it. In every initial case, that's been the case; which drew me to the conclusion that a simple reporting of a missing person was next to useless, so to give the police a fair shake; I upped the ante, to see if they could solve a crime with clues. Therefore, I had Brooke call *911* and, sure enough, she provided a clue that connected her to McIntyre—a warehouse. I provided the second clue connecting the two—the thirty-six-hour window. That should have provided sufficient information for them to locate her in time; but no, Hardwick had to shift his focus to finding *me*. And that's where the dissimilarities with other cities truly began." He laughed shortly, "I do have to give Hardwick credit though. He did some fine detective work there. He nearly had me ensnared. The difference here is that detectives in the other cities focused on using the massive clues provided and got to their second or third victim with hours to spare."

Daniel sighed again, "Okay, third victim here in Atlanta. I'm going to assume that someone overlooked a key location simply because they drew an incorrect assumption. Still, even had the office had not messed up, there was still no detecting going on. I all but told them that Sequoia Richardson was in a parking structure; so, in truth, it was just an all-out manhunt? Now, looking back at every city I've been in, it's been the same. Give the police a chance to do their job, and when they fail, I feed them a tiny nibble to see if they can succeed. When they fail again, I turn it into no more than a manhunt requiring no policing skills at all. I've done no good. What I can't fathom is how I didn't see this before."

Daniel slapped himself hard on the head, winced, and then did it again, "I got derailed somewhere along the line. What started out as a test of police competency after failing to find my wife's murderer has turned into no more than my own murder spree. I must find a way to shift it back, to find my purpose again. I'm not a killer, I'm a scientist; and I have to make my experiments mean something again; make the deaths purposeful."

He checked the man lying on the floor once more, to ensure he was in a deep sleep, "It would be easier to simply use you, but I don't think you're important enough to the APD; I think they need to care about the victim to make a truly phenomenal effort. Time to get to work."

CHAPTER 27

I t's been four days," Hardwick observed, pouring a cup of coffee before heading toward a chair in the little commissary, "and not a peep out of Price."

"Maybe the bastard's moved on," Wilson offered, moving to pour his own cup.

"Nah, he's just yanking us," Harding said before shoving the rest of a muffin in his mouth.

"Yeah, that's the impression I'm getting," Cortez added, taking a sip of his apple juice. "I think the sick son-of-a-bitch is playing us. Making us suffer for letting Richardson die."

"He's a son-of-a-bitch all right, and he's out there, right now, planning some major retribution," Harding concurred, "and it ain't gonna be pretty."

"You don't think he's done with the APD then?" Wilson replied, settling at the table with his oatmeal and coffee. "I mean, doesn't he usually quit each city after three victims?"

Hardwick shook his head, "Yeah, that's been his M.O., but we screwed up the last one, remember? I don't think he's going to forgive us that one. No, I think Harding is right. He's working on something else, and I think this time he's not going to be so forthcoming with the details needed to find the victim so easily."

"You think that last find was easy?" Wilson blurted.

"Way harder than it should have been," Cortez snapped. "We should have found Richardson easy, and if we had, this nut job would be out of our lives."

"Yeah, but not out of commission altogether; he'd still be out there doing the same thing to precincts in other cities," Hardwick replied sharply.

"Yeah, and I'd be shouting a good riddance and then happily send a "sorry that it's your turn" gift basket to the precinct that gets him next," Cortez retorted.

"We all know it's best if we're the ones that nail him. We need this after the Richardson fiasco. The other precincts may have solved case number three in their jurisdiction; but they never caught the guy," Hardwick countered.

"I don't think they really tried," Harding added. "Like

us, I think they just wanted the guy gone; their cities returned to some sort of normalcy."

"Do you remember how mad he got when I shifted the search focus to him?" Hardwick asked suddenly.

"Yeah, he was pissed all right," Harding laughed. "I think you got too close for his comfort."

"Precisely," Hardwick replied thoughtfully.

"What are you thinking?" Wilson asked.

"I'm thinking we stop playing marionettes for this puppeteer. The next time he calls in, we go back to being detectives and we locate the perp. We stop him, we stop this insanity."

"What about the victims?" Cortez asked. "Do we just let him keep killing until we catch him?"

"No, we put black and whites on the search while we do what we do best."

"Bring down the bad guys," Cortez grinned.

"Damned straight," Harding snapped, slapping his hand on the table.

"Am I missing something?" Wilson interrupted. "We followed that technique with Brooke Madison, but she still died, so how is it going to be a better plan this time around?"

"Do you ever really listen to full conversations before making asinine comments?" Harding retorted. "Hardwick just said that we nearly caught the son-of-a-bitch during the Madison case, or weren't you listening to that part?"

"He's back," the captain called from the doorway, preventing Wilson from responding to Harding. As he followed his fellow detectives from the commissary, Wilson wondered whether they'd finally met their match and if there was any possible way of stopping Christian Price at all. After all, no other police force had been able to. What Wilson didn't realize was that Hardwick was pondering along the very same lines.

CHAPTER 28

Daniel once again parked along the curb outside the district 5 Headquarters, beneath his favorite oak: observing the officers comings and goings. For the past four days, he'd researched ideas, fought with himself, and did more research, all with the intent of devising the perfect murder with his few remaining supplies or with none of his supplies at all.

In the end, he'd formulated a scheme that would require only his sleeping mixture and some duct tape—for the most part. The only hitch in his design was accessing a particularly high security area—of which he was observing right now. He glanced down at the schematics he'd procured online. If he could reach his desired destination within this building, he might just be able to pull this off; and he was determined to make it work, so he'd find a way to reach his ideal locale.

He'd also waited this long because he wanted the APD to think he'd moved on, so that they'd relax their guard and send their officers back to their routine patrols.

As for his victim of choice? He'd already selected her; but he couldn't abduct her until all was set in motion; until everything was in place and his plan ready to execute. With his pulse pounding, he reached for the brand-new toolbox he'd purchased just that morning, stepped from his car, and made his way toward the APD headquarters.

"Hey," he muttered to himself as he walked down the sidewalk, "I'm Daniel and I'm entering the lion's den. There's got to be some psychological significance here." He restrained himself from laughing aloud at the parallel between his situation and the Bible story, but he still found it amusing enough to plaster a smile on his face.

He grinned widely, nodding boldly at the passing officers as he pulled open the door that would lead him where he never thought he would go.

"Help you?" The desk sergeant asked immediately.

"Elevator maintenance," Daniel replied simply.

The sergeant nodded and then returned his attention to his paperwork.

Morons like you are why people die, Daniel said tacitly. *You could have at least verified my credentials, inspected my toolbox...anything to prove I am who I say I am.*

After a moment, he decided that, once again, fortune must be willing his experiments to succeed, or things would never go perfectly for him. He then quickly determined it was best not to tempt fate and headed toward the stairwell, reviewing in his mind the schematics he'd memorized.

He only hoped he was easily able to access the pit where the safety buffer for the elevator car was located, or he'd be headed back out the front door; his idea scrapped, and a new search started for another scheme.

However, reaching his destination was only the beginning in this instance, because once he determined whether this plan was doable, he would only have an exceedingly small window—a matter of hours—in which to set everything up, including the victim. This vicinity was simply too high risk to allow for too much passage of time. The longer he was in the building...he shook the thought of capture from his mind. He couldn't afford to allow stress and nerves to draw attention to his presence.

A few minutes later, he approached the small closet-sized room, near the base of the elevator shaft. A quick inspection discovered little space for maneuvering, which meant he'd have to work with the door open and start praying that no one came down here.

He pulled open the small metal latch that accessed the actual shaft and sighed. If he thought the closet was a tight space...this room made the closet look like a stadium. To accomplish what he needed to accomplish; he was going to have to make some alterations.

With a quick glance down the corridor to ensure he was still alone, he opened his toolbox and retrieved a keyhole saw, then settled on his knees and started sawing through the sheetrock around the latch; thankful once more that the pit wasn't housed in concrete or brick—although he'd come prepared for that also.

Half-hour later, he pushed the sheetrock aside and maneuvered through the hole he'd made. He looked up and saw the elevator car high up the shaft. A quick inspection of the pit revealed what he was searching for —the buffer.

The buffer is the spring-rod protrusion that prevents the elevator from impacting the concrete flooring on the lowest level. It also provides a buffer between the car and the passengers, preventing an annoying jarring sensation each time it stops.

Daniel sat back and waited until the elevator descended and tap the buffer firmly, but gently. He grinned. "This is perfect," he purred, noting the distance between the car and the walls. He'd need to be precise, or the elevator could jar the equipment he set up, and that wouldn't do at all.

The elevator sat for a few minutes longer and then started its slow ascent.

"Time to get started," he murmured. He reached back and retrieved the items he'd need from his toolbox.

CHAPTER 29

An hour later, his work interrupted several times by the arrival of the elevator car, Daniel closed the toolbox, and then set about inspecting his work for flaws. The coming and going of the car had annoyed him initially, but after the third decent, he used it to his advantage—using the time to examine and adjust his set up.

With a satisfied smile, he left the closet, closed the door, and headed back up the corridor. Now to set the next phase of his plan into motion: convincing the desk sergeant that he'd need to return later in the day to complete his work.

He reached the lobby and approached the front desk.

"Excuse me," he said, when the sergeant didn't acknowledge his presence immediately.

"Yeah, what can I do for you? Oh, maintenance guy."

"Yeah, that's right. Listen. There's a bolt that needs replacing, but I didn't have the right type in my toolbox, so I'm going to need to go get one and come back."

"It's nearing rush hour. You'll be stuck in traffic for some time if you try to maneuver around at this time of day."

Daniel laughed shortly, "Yeah, don't I know it, but if I don't complete it today, my day off tomorrow becomes a workday."

"Ah, hell no! If it were me, I'd sprout wings to get it done."

"Damn straight! Hey, are you going to be here next shift? Or am I going to have to go through the same hassle I went through with you to get to where I need to be?" Daniel framed the question as a joke, but he really needed to know. After all, this guy was easy to by-pass, whereas another sergeant might not be.

The front desk sergeant laughed, "Nah, I'll be here, and I promise, no cavity searches this time."

Daniel laughed, more from relief at the response than the actual intended humor, "I'll see you in a few."

"Okay, I ain't going anywhere."

Daniel headed out the front door, grinning as wide as his lips allowed. *Too easy,* he thought, forcing himself to walk and not skip with glee to his car.

"Next, we sit and wait for the arrival of our victim."

CHAPTER 30

It was nearing 7 p.m. when he spotted the young woman, he'd been watching for the past four days, headed up the sidewalk to the police precinct. The streets were nearly empty, for which he was thankful. Atlantians that worked in the city long abandoned the area at the end of the workday, and those who'd be returning to enjoy Atlanta's nightlife, shouldn't be close by here.

He stepped from the car as she approached his vehicle, ready to intercept her. For this plan to work, he needed her cooperation—even if he used coercion to elicit said cooperation. This was one time in which chloroform, or his sleep elixir, wouldn't be useful.

As soon as Daniel decided that it would have to be an

APD officer abducted, he'd watched and waited for the perfect woman working third shift and was elated when he'd spotted Lucia Mendocino on his first night's watch. For the next three days, as he researched the perfect murder, he also researched Officer Mendocino's life. It saddened him that she had a family; a six-month-old baby boy among them, but the APD needed to feel the enormity of his resolve, and if they really cared about their own—more than the public—then they'd find her and return her to her son.

What he needed to prevent now was her fighting back or alerting nearby pedestrians, few as they were, before he explained the direness of her circumstance.

She'd just made it past the hood of his car, when he stealthily approached from the rear and wrapped an arm about her neck, a switchblade pressed against her back, "Don't squirm. I don't want you dead, or your baby boy," he said quickly in case she had some martial arts training and decided to flip him onto the sidewalk.

Lucia went rigid at the mention of her son, not even attempting to struggle.

"Good. We're going to go sit in this car over here and have a chat." He tugged against her neck, pulling her backwards toward the rear passenger door of his BMW. He increased the pressure on her neck when he lowered the switchblade, "I need to open the car door. If you try to escape, I'll snap your neck, which means your baby boy loses his mom."

He reached down, opened the car door, and shoved her inside, following quickly behind.

Her eyes widened when she saw him, and he grinned.

"You're not wearing a mask, which means you're..."

"...going to kill you?" He concluded with a laugh. In fact, he didn't need to wear a mask, because he'd long ago changed his appearance to where he didn't resemble Christian Price in the least; nor would he resemble this man after tonight, should Lucia survive to provide a description. "No, Lucia. I'm not going to kill you. Only two circumstances are possible in which death will occur in this scenario. Would you like to know what they are?"

Lucia nodded, and Daniel smiled, "I thought you might. The first potential death will be your son, and that will only happen if you do not follow my dictates this evening to the letter. If you attempt to behave in any manner other than your normal self, my associate will kill your son. If you attempt to signal anyone overtly that you are in distress, my associate will kill your son. I don't need to speak to anyone, just press speed dial. If my associate's phone rings even once, your son dies. And before you think that you'll be able to signal in some manner by behaving differently, know that I've been watching you for the past week, so I know your normal behavior around your work mates." Daniel was laughing inside at her reaction and the tears streaming down her face. He'd convinced her well enough that his associate, which of course didn't exist, would end her son's life should she mess up; and the implication was all he needed. He let that sink in and then continued, "So, I guess you need to ask yourself—do you consider yourself a good enough actress to deceive your co-workers?"

She nodded, unable to speak past the fear paralyzing her vocal cords. Daniel moved to exit the car, which caused Lucia to find her voice, "You said there were two scenarios."

"I did, didn't I? Nice catch," Daniel replied softly. "There are, but you won't be privy to the second potential dying circumstance just yet. I promise, however, not to keep you on tenterhooks for long. Let's get inside the precinct and ensure your son's survival in round one, and then I'll reveal what you need to do next and the potential person you'll save by following my instructions to a tee. After all, if this first part goes awry...well, there won't be a need to move on to part two. Ok?"

Lucia nodded.

"Good, let's begin, shall we? You'll precede me into the precinct and then stop in the corridor at the stair-well. Once there, wait for me to join you. I'm trusting that you'll be able to accomplish this without need of handholding. For your son?"

Lucia nodded again and Daniel slid from the car. He reached in and retrieved his toolbox, and then offered Lucia a hand. He squeezed it reassuringly. The action was so gentlemanly, it caused her to tear up.

"Dry your eyes please," Daniel whispered harshly, "and chin up."

She swiped at her eyes and wiped her nose on her sleeve.

"Now, after you."

Although he was convinced that this first-year rookie would obey his every command, he still walked close behind her. When she reached for the door, he whispered close to her ear, "Academy Award performance."

She nodded slightly, pulled open the door, and headed inside. Daniel expected the front desk sergeant to acknowledge her presence at least, but apparently, the comings and goings of the officers was so frequent that it warranted no more than a glance; however, he did acknowledge Daniel's return.

"See you managed to sprout those wings," he quipped.

"Determination for a day off is a great motivator," Daniel laughed. His peripheral focus homed in on Lucia, as she moved down the corridor. He smiled inwardly when he saw her stop, as instructed. "Well, the sooner I get that bolt replaced, the sooner I end my day and start my day off. I'll see you on the way out."

"Sure thing."

He moved down the corridor and opened the door swiftly, silently bidding Lucia to precede him into the stairwell. "Head to the lowest level, to the storage area," he instructed, following her at a short distance, so that, should they pass anyone, there would not be a presumption they were together. He may intend to change his appearance as soon as he walked free of this building, but that didn't mean he wanted to take unnecessary chances.

Not surprisingly, they didn't pass a soul, as most people preferred to use the elevator to the stairs nowadays, and even fewer people had cause to visit the storage area, where unused office equipment sat awaiting the day when someone would have use of it again.

When he reached the closet that led to the elevator pit, he ushered Lucia inside; and then reached into his toolbox and withdrew some duct tape.

"Okay, you will be happy to know that your son will remain safe now. Does that make you happy?"

Lucia immediately broke into shoulder-shaking, body-wracking tears. Daniel looked down the corridor to ensure that her breakdown wasn't drawing undue attention. When he saw that they remained alone, he allowed her to cry for a few minutes. When she started drawing in jagged breaths, he knew her crying spell was drawing to a close.

"Okay, now that you've had your moment, it's time to go over the second potential death circumstance in this scenario. Are you ready for me to explain?"

Lucia nodded, wide-eyed with terror as he ripped off some of the duct tape and placed it over her mouth.

"Okay, this is how part two is going to go," he explained slowly, as he tore another longer strip of duct tape and wound it about her wrists behind her back. "Your officers and detectives have been on the hunt for the serial killer, Christian Price, correct?"

Lucia nodded and her eyes went from wide to bug-eyed. He didn't resemble the sketch that had been circulating, so she didn't connect him to Price when they were in her car. She thought that she was in danger because he wasn't masked, which meant she could identify him; now, however, it was different, because Price was a known murderer.

"That's right, Lucia, I'm Christian Price, which means, I've chosen you for my next victim."

Lucia forgot all about remaining calm and started squealing, struggling against her bindings. Daniel couldn't afford for this last experiment to go awry, so he smacked her hard upside the head, "Settle down now," he commanded firmly. She moaned against the duct tape as a loud ringing started in her ears.

"Now," he continued, "you should be happy to know that you have the best chance for survival because I'm going to make certain that I give them some good clues to find you, okay?"

Lucia didn't respond this time. She sat immobile, her gaze glazing over in shock.

Daniel decided that she understood well enough and moved to complete setting up. He pulled a syringe from his coat pocket and slid the needle into the vein in Lucia's arm, watching with satisfaction as her eyes rolled back into her head, and she fell into a deep sleep.

Before he could finalize her placement inside the pit however, he needed to ensure that he provided Detective Hardwick the pertinent instructions needed to prevent Lucia's imminent death. It would be a sad turn of events if he placed her inside the shaft only to have her die before...he picked up his disposable cell and dialed the front desk sergeant, grinning at the irony of this call.

Atlanta Police Department, Zone 5.

"This is Christian Price..."

Hold and I'll put you through, the sergeant interrupted, and Daniel's smile widened. As the minutes ticked by, waiting for Hardwick to answer his call, his mind began racing: Had they discovered his whereabouts and were closing in on him while he held on the line? Had they found a way to trace his phone? Just before Daniel determined that it would be best to disconnect the call, Hardwick came on the line.

Detective Hardwick here. We thought you'd tucked tail and run.

"It took you a long time to answer. I nearly gave up on you."

We were down in the commissary. We needed time to get back to the bullpen.

Relief flooded through Daniel's body, and he sighed. *Time to get to it then*, he thought and then brought the conversation around to business, "I'll not remain on the line long, Detective, since I'm incredibly angry at the loss of Miss Richardson. She was all but handed to you on a silver platter."

If it helps any, our captain put the two detectives responsible on administrative leave and both will be terminated after a cursory investigation.

"Well, I can't say I'm disappointed that they'll be looking elsewhere for employment, as they were far too incompetent to be police officers, but aren't you going to take any responsibility this time, Hardwick? After all, you ignored my call, which could have…"

Anti-venom is precise. The paramedics wouldn't have had it on their vehicle...

"Fine, point taken," Price interrupted. "I'll make this easy and difficult at the same time. You see, I came to the realization that you and your co-workers weren't required to do any detecting."

That single comment had Hardwick's pulse racing, as if the man were somehow privy to their conversations. Did Price know that he and his fellow detectives planned to pursue him instead of participating in this next search? He shook his head and tried to focus on what Price was saying.

"However, since I have neither the inclination, nor the time, to test your detecting skills at this point in the game, I'm simply giving you unlimited time in which to locate one of your officers; however, I won't be providing but a single clue."

Wait! What do you mean, "locate one of your officers"?

"That one sentence is what you latch onto? No surprise there. Yes, I've abducted one of your own. Hopefully, that will ensure a better response than civilians seem to warrant."

We did everything we could...

"Save your breath, Detective, and listen well because I'll only say this once. You have half an hour to kill the power that feeds the businesses along Spring Street...oh wait, they've renamed much of that street Ted Turner Drive. Well nonetheless, you get the idea. If you fail to convince the powers that be of the necessity of killing the electricity, then your officer will surely die, since she's connected to an electrical device in a building along that section of road. The longer you keep the electricity off, the longer you have to search for her, which translates to a longer lifespan for your officer. Of course, the longer it takes you to find her, the longer the citizens that live or work along that stretch will go without electricity. So, detective, I do hope you can persuade whoever needs to be persuaded, that this officer's life is worth the inconvenience to the populace. Your thirty minutes starts now."

Daniel disconnected the call and checked the time on his watch. It would take approximately fifteen minutes to get Lucia's body into the pit, position her, and set up the IV drip meant to keep her sedated for a good long while. He settled against the wall and watched the minutes tick by, but the lights remained on. When the time reached his fifteen-minute set up deadline, he reached in his toolbox and pulled out his flashlight. He didn't need it now, but he was hoping that he would, before the thirty-minute deadline was reached. If they didn't turn off the electricity as instructed, he would simply take a ride in the elevator to ensure Lucia died quickly. Then he'd be ensured that she'd be found, eventually—through the stench of decaying flesh.

He took a deep breath, then reached down and started scooting Lucia's body toward the opening in the sheetrock. He looked up to ensure that the elevator was high enough up the shaft to work undeterred. He certainly didn't want them both getting squashed if this took too long, or the electricity remained on. Next, he propped her up against the buffer and bent her head to lay it across the top of it. He snorted softly when her head wouldn't bend quite as far as he needed.

He grabbed her legs and repositioned her into more of a recline position, and then tested the head bend again. This time, her head cocked exactly right, so that her temple lay nearly flat against the buffer. He checked his watch, though he really wasn't in a huge hurry. Still, it concerned him slightly that the lights were still blazing with only minutes remaining in his deadline. That realization had him moving more swiftly, as he needed to be out of the shaft and well on his way before the search efforts began.

With one hand on her head to hold it in place, he reached down to retrieve his duct tape; then used his teeth to loosen a strip. He latched that end to her cheek, and then held it in place securely while unraveling more tape. The pull of each strip was like thunder to his ears in the confined space, but he needed to ensure that she stayed put; so, he wrapped the first strip around her head and then around the pole; then began again swiftly, until it looked more like a giant ball of grey tape than a head.

When he'd used every inch of tape, he sat back and inspected his work rapidly; shaking her firmly, tugging and pulling on her head—all to make certain that she wouldn't be able to pull herself free. He tilted his head and looked at her, his face twisting into a comical grin. The only way anyone would be able to identify this ball as human was by the mouth and nose—the only two features that remained visible beneath the giant wad.

Another glance at his watch showed he had less than two minutes remaining before deadline. He went to strap her arms to her body, but then realized that he'd used all his duct tape. He sighed and crawled partway back through the hole in the wall, reaching for the other roll. As with her head, he loosened some tape, placed the sticky end to one arm and held it firmly while pulling more tape from the roll; then started wrapping it around and around her torso. Now he was confident, that should the drip run out, prior to the detectives locating her, she'd be unable to move or cry out. Next, he retrieved the needle attached to the IV bag that he'd set up earlier in the day, slid it into her arm, and duct taped it in place.

Just as he reached up to set the knob to a precisely slow drip, the power went off. He smiled widely, "Well, at least you won't die before I exit the building."

He reached over to retrieve his flashlight and concluded his work by the glare of a halogen bulb. "You may survive after all," he whispered close to her head and then slipped back through the hole he'd cut. Without delay, he collected all his gear and headed back up the stairs.

"Hey, what's with the power?" He asked the front desk sergeant when he reached the lobby.

"Nothing. Just a power outage. It'll be back on before long. Did you get your work done?"

"Yeah, just in the nick of time," Daniel replied honestly.

"Glad to hear it. Enjoy your day off."

"Thanks. I hope you don't have to work in the dark too long," Daniel replied amicably, and pushed open the front door of the building. "Have a good night."

"You too."

Daniel walked outside and headed toward his car; but the first thing he noticed was that some of the power, further down Ted Turner Drive was still on. "Must be racing to cut power at individual substations," he said to himself. "Oh well, not my concern, as long as the power along this stretch stays off. Now, I need to inform citizens of the true reason for the power outage. Don't want the APD getting lazy."

He placed the toolbox into his car and settled into the driver's seat, then pulled out his disposable cell and dialed the Channel 5 Newsroom.

CHAPTER 31

Thirty-five minutes prior to lights out

H e's back," the captain called from the door of the commissary and all four detectives, and the captain, took off for the bullpen at a dead run.

"Start a trace," he snapped at his fellow detectives. Cortez veered off and headed for his phone.

Detective Hardwick wasted no time in punching the only blinking light, followed quickly by the speaker button.

"Detective Hardwick here. We thought you'd tucked tail and run."

"It took you a long time to answer. I nearly gave up on you."

"We were down in the commissary. We needed time to get back to the bullpen."

The call proceeded, with all men listening intently for anything that might assist in providing a clue as to their officer's whereabouts. One thing that none of them missed this time, however, was that Hardwick did nothing to agitate Price. No snapping, no baiting comments—nothing. That meant only one thing: Hardwick was worried.

The captain sat in on much of the conversation with Price, but as soon as Price mentioned cutting the power, he left for his office.

The moment Price concluded the call, Hardwick slammed his finger against the speaker button, "Tell me we got him!"

Cortez shook his head and sighed heavily, "I'm being told that we can't trace a burner, unless we were to geolocate it by accessing his GPS or his Wi-Fi signal. There simply wasn't enough time."

"Shit!" Hardwick yelled, slamming his fist against his desk. He drew in a deep breath through his nostrils, "Let's see if the captain's made headway."

All four detectives filed into the captain's office. The captain looked up and questioned Cortez with a nod. Cortez shook his head, and it was the captain's turn to draw in a deep, agitated breath. He listened to the person on the other end a minute longer then responded.

"That's correct, Governor, and only you can make it happen. It's imperative that you..." he stopped talking when the governor interrupted him and then he interrupted the governor, "This isn't a terrorist attack, sir; this is a serial killer who's now got one of our own. If we don't kill the power, he'll ensure she dies within the next half an hour. How is that going to look come election time? We're already struggling in the eyes of the citizenry..."

The captain's tirade was interrupted again, but when he hung up the phone a minute later, he appeared satisfied, "The governor is calling the Department of Energy now to ensure that power is cut; however, he sadly regrets that he may not be able to see it done in only half hour."

"Twenty-nine minutes now, actually," Wilson said, and his cheeks reddened at the looks he received. "Sorry," he muttered.

"That's a habit you better break, Wilson," the captain snarled, "because I swear that if you point out the time to me one more time, I'm going to personally ensure you're demoted to beat cop. Time to get this search started —again."

The captain picked up the phone and gave the front

desk sergeant the instructions on calling in all officers, whether on duty or not. It didn't take long for them to arrive, as everyone had been told to remain on alert until the Christian Price fiasco blew over with certainty. Just as everyone was filing into the auditorium, the lights went out.

"I guess that means the governor got through ok," Harding said, pulling out his flashlight.

"Hopefully, the Department of Energy will keep the power off until we locate our missing officer," Cortez added, flicking his own flashlight on.

"Hopefully, we'll find our missing officer before Price kills her," Hardwick said softly and then all went to the auditorium to instruct the officers on their latest search parameters. None were aware that in the lowest level of their very own building, Lucia Mendocino was strapped to the elevator buffer; and should her co-workers fail to locate her before the electricity was turned back on, her head would be decimated, like a watermelon with a sledgehammer.

CHAPTER 32

Christian arrived back at the Highland Park Apartment Complex and did his normal sweep of the building before parking and heading toward the apartment that he currently occupied. He had his syringe in hand ready to administer the next dose of sleep aid as soon as he walked in. The last thing he needed was for his latest captive to awaken too soon.

He pushed open the door, and immediately noticed that the floor inside the front door was deserted; his prey gone. Panic set in but subsided quickly when heard retching sounds emanating from the bathroom. He sighed inwardly, and tip-toed quickly in that direction.

"Obviously, I've misjudged the dosage for such a

hefty male," he whispered to himself. "Well, I'll just get you sleeping again and then I'll go back for another syringe."

He paused at the bathroom door, slightly ajar, and peered around the side. He needed to make certain that he was facing away from him; otherwise, if he felt strong enough, he could easily barrel attack and incapacitate him. With the difference in their sizes, Christian wouldn't stand a chance.

He was kneeling over the edge of the toilet, his back to the door, the heaving sounds causing bile to rise in Christian's throat. He needed to deal with this swiftly, if for no other reason than to shut him up.

He slipped inside, mentally calculated the location of any vein in the neck, and jammed the needle in, depressing the liquid into his body swiftly. The man flailed at his assault, but only briefly. Within seconds, the Melatonin and Rohypnol worked their magic, sending the muscular male into the arms of oblivion. He slid sideways and conked his head onto the tile flooring.

Daniel immediately returned to the living area to retrieve another syringe. He then returned to the bathroom, lifted his huge, limp arm and delivered another dose. He wouldn't make the same mistake again and risk him waking during one of his outings.

He bent to place his arms beneath the unconscious man's armpits, so he could remove him from the bathroom floor, but after tugging several minutes without making any headway, he gave up.

"You can stay there," he muttered and then headed back to the living room. He was more interested in learning what was happening with his current abduction, than worrying overly much about the comfort of the person with whom he was merely residing with temporarily.

He flipped on the television and immediately settled onto the couch to watch the breaking news on Channel 5. The first thing that caught his attention was the map behind the anchor's head that displayed the area affected by the blackout.

If you live in the blackout area, police are asking that you remain patient while they complete their search of all facilities along Ted Turner Drive.

That's right, Charles, Patricia Wheaton continued, *especially as this isn't just any ordinary blackout. A little more than half an hour ago, a call came into the station from serial killer, Christian Price, informing us that he'd abducted yet another Atlanta citizen.*

Not just any citizen, Patricia, Charles interjected. *This time, Price abducted one of the Atlanta Police Department's own officers; and according to Price, the life of that officer is dependent upon whether the power remains off. Right now, we're going live to the scene outside the Atlanta's Zone 5 headquarters, where our reporter in the field, Cassandra Bouchard, is standing by with an update. Cassandra?*

Thank you, Charles. I'm standing outside of APD's Zone 5, where, what appears to be, the bulk of this zone's officers are pulling out en masse, heading to begin, presumably, a search of every building lining the entirety of Ted Turner Drive. The only reason we can ascertain their intent is because of the call we received from the perpetrator.

Cassandra? The anchorwoman interjected.

Yes, Patricia.

Have you been able to discuss with anyone yet on what type of power source the officer is connected to? Why the need to have the power off in such a large coverage area?

Unfortunately, no, Patricia. Police have cordoned off the area directly surrounding Zone 5 to keep reporters from blocking access to and from the building; and up until just a few moments ago, all officers were hole up inside, presumably discussing how to approach this latest assault by serial killer, Christian Price.

Thank you, Cassandra. Let us know if there's anything more to report from the scene.

So, as of right now, Charles Braxton continued as the

camera faded from Cassandra Bouchard, *all police appear to know is that one of their officers is being held in a location...*

Daniel hit the mute button and moved to the kitchen to collect a snack. There wasn't anything more he could do right now but wait.

CHAPTER 33

Half hour prior to the live news broadcast

W e should take role call to see who's missing," Cortez stated as the detectives followed the captain to the auditorium where all officers were supposed to have reported moments prior.

"You don't think that will be a waste of time? We know it's one of ours..."

"Yeah, but we don't know who," Cortez persisted.

"True, but taking roll may not provide us that answer," Hardwick interjected. "We all know that when we do an all-out call for officers to report, there are a few off-duty officers that decide that the order doesn't apply to them. So, if we take precious time away from the investigation to do a roll call, all we'll accomplish is to find out whose ducking duty."

"Except the one that's tied up somewhere," Wilson added. "Do you really think some will ditch, knowing it's one of our own on the line?"

"I think that selfishness knows no bounds," Cortez mused.

"Precisely," Hardwick replied, with a shake of his head, "so let's focus on our job right now."

The captain climbed the stairs to the podium and the auditorium fell silent.

"Since we are completely in the dark—pardon the pun—on precisely which type of electrical device Price has our officer connected to, it's imperative that we not overlook anything. Every officer is to inspect every nook and cranny in every building; and there better not be any officer making presumptions that could lead to this officer's death. I better be crystal clear on that point. When I say every nook and cranny, I mean every nook and cranny. I don't care if the nook is small enough to house a mouse, it better get checked. If there is a power source attached to a building that entire building will be swept from top to bottom, inside and out. We all know what this maniac is capable of doing, so we are not to overlook any possibilities. Now, I'm going to divide everyone into two divisions. Division one will start on the Northwest end of Ted Turner Drive and the other is to start on the Southwest end. We'll meet in the middle; hopefully with our officer in tow."

"What about the part of Spring Street that wasn't renamed? Do we check there?" One of the officers called out the question from the back row.

"Damn," the captain muttered beneath his breath, tossing a glance toward his detectives. He shook his head and closed his eyes for a moment, sighing heavily. He'd forgotten there was still a small snippet of Spring Street that the city council hadn't renamed yet after the media mogul, Ted Turner. He was also grateful that he held to the belief that no question was too stupid to ask. "You're right," he called, "he may decide to throw us a curve ball. Good catch. The last thing we need to do is presume that he'll restrict his location to the renamed section alone. So, I believe Spring Street is still Spring from Ivan Allen to West Peachtree. So, in reality we'll have four divisions working the grid; four cars each division."

"Should we bother checking stand-along parking structures?" Another officer called out.

"Yes," the captain answered, thinking that that really *was* a stupid question, although he kept that opinion to himself. "Most parking structures have some form of electrical usage—lights, ticketing booths, maintenance closets. Remember people, you're not to bypass any building—and I mean any building—that has a source of power running to it. Is everyone clear on what we're trying to accomplish here?" Voices called out understanding, nearly simultaneously. "Good, because this search is going to be foot patrol—primarily. Detective Hardwick will explain how this is going to go down."

"Okay," Hardwick said, replacing the captain at the podium, "There's going to be a single driver per group of officers. We don't need the street flooded with patrol cars, just cops. When each group of four cars reaches the starting point, officers in the first two cars will debark and begin the sweep. Car one will tackle the buildings on the left; car two, the buildings on the right. After officers have cleared the first building on each side of the street, officers in the next two cars will debark and do a second sweep of those buildings. Each division will continue in that manner until we meet up in the middle; and, as the captain said, hopefully, we'll find our officer along the way. Any more questions before we divide up and head out?" No one stood or shouted out. "Good."

"Spring Street Division. You'll head out first. Eight cars, eight drivers. Four at each end..." he paused, pointing his flashlight at the first eight officers seated in the front row. "Grab keys and vehicles. Your search parties will meet up with you in a minute. As soon as those men ran from the room, he pointed his flashlight to another eight officers, "You four are drivers. Ted Turner Northwest end. And you four are drivers too. Southwest end. The eight officers jumped up and ran for the parking garage.

"Okay, the rest of you, grab your gear and flashlights. You'll be searching the buildings. Meet up with the drivers. Four or five to a car. Go."

The captain and his four detectives watched the men sprint from the room.

"What are we going to do?" Wilson asked. "We can't exactly do anything productive with the computers down. Think we should hit the streets too? We certainly shouldn't sit here twiddling our..."

"Hey, bright bulb," Cortez interjected. "We're standing in one of the buildings in the search grid."

"Ah come on," Wilson retorted, "You don't really think that Price had the *cajones* or the capabilities to infiltrate our facility to convey a hostage beneath the noses of a hundred plus police officers, do you?"

"Not really, no," Cortez conceded.

"Thank you for your honesty," Wilson said sardonically.

"That doesn't mean we shouldn't search," Cortez added.

Before Wilson could lob another retort, the captain interrupted, "It doesn't matter what we think, Wilson.

What matters is that we do our jobs. Even if it we feel the probability is low that Price could get in and out without detection, hostage in tow, we may as well certify ourselves as village idiots if we don't conduct a thorough search."

"Price isn't stupid," Hardwick interjected. "In fact, the level of his self-dubbed experiments is downright genius..." Hardwick trailed off, which caught the attention of his fellow detectives.

"What're you thinking, Hardwick?" Harding asked.

"He called himself a scientist," Hardwick said thoughtfully.

"When?" the captain asked.

"You weren't there," Hardwick commented abstractly. "It was during our first phone conversation. He likened himself to a scientist conducting experiments on rats."

"Okay, and?" Wilson asked, uncertain where this line of thought was leading. "I fail to see how this is pertinent. Most criminals can draw a parallel between themselves and a profession of consequence. It seems to help them justify their actions."

"Yes, but what if he really is a scientist?" Cortez asked Hardwick in an Aha tone.

"Precisely," Hardwick continued. "Damn it. The power had to be off right now."

"Okay, let's say he really is a scientist. How does this help us?" Wilson continued to argue.

"If the power weren't off, we could conduct more intensive research on Price's dead wife." Harding stated emphatically.

"Precisely," Hardwick continued. "Knowledge is power, right? So, let's say that my intellectual spark proves true—that Price is a scientist. That will give us more insight into the person and give us new search parameters. The more we know, the better chance we have of finding and stopping him; however, since the power is off, we'll have to conduct a search and do our research later. Hopefully, we find our officer and conduct the search before he flees our jurisdiction."

"We may not have to wait," the captain interjected, his own tone thoughtful. "This building has a separate backup power source. We can turn on the juice here, in our precinct, without affecting the buildings within the search grid."

"And if this particular genius did manage to slip a victim in beneath our noses? Aren't we putting our officer at risk?" Wilson argued.

Hardwick nodded, "Yes, but I think that we're all in agreement that it's a tiny likelihood. As you said, Wilson, he'd have to have some serious *cajones* to slip a victim beneath our noses. Not to mention the ability.

Remember when we determined that we four would do some actual detecting while the others conducted a search? We need to catch this guy, and sooner rather than later. We've actually been handed the perfect opportunity: a cooperative mayor, a limited and precise search grid, and an unlimited amount of time."

"It doesn't take four detectives and a captain to do research," the captain interjected, "but I get where you're going. Does anyone have any further objections to this before I head down to the generator room?"

Everyone shook his head, "Good. Hardwick, as soon as the lights come on, you hit the computers, since this was your brain baby. The rest of us will do a sweep of the building. That way, we're still getting the job done while getting our real jobs done. Let's go!"

CHAPTER 34

Daniel finished washing his snack dishes and moved back to the living room to see whether his new favorite reporter, Cassandra Bouchard, had any further news to impart related to the frantic search for the APD officer.

He was so certain that the Atlanta PD would succeed this time that he wanted to go ahead and pack up his gear and be prepared to leave the moment the news broke about the successful outcome. The joy in his step faltered, however, as he moved around to the front of the television set.

Cassandra Bouchard was indeed back on air, reporting, but that wasn't what caught his attention; rather it was the lights burning inside the precinct. He fell onto the couch, his face twisted in comical horror.

"Son-of-a-bitch," he whispered to himself. What he wanted to do was scream at the top of his lungs, but he knew better than to draw attention to himself. "Has the Atlanta PD completely lost their senses?"

He picked up his cell and dialed the Channel 5 newsroom, but before the call connected, he hit *end* and tossed the phone onto the couch next to him. "No! You'll receive no more help from me," he snarled. He shook his head and drew in several deep breaths through his nostrils. The anger rampaging through his system was deeper and stronger than at any other time in his life; except for when the Chicago PD discovered his wife's body.

"I now know with certainty," he whispered, shaking his head slowly, the anger displaced by a slow deepening sorrow, "that I could remain in Atlanta for the remainder of my life, kidnapping woman after woman, and would watch each die. It sickens me to know that, despite every effort to make your job easier; to try to lift the officers here from a listless state, I have failed miserably; and because I have failed, Lucia Mendocino will die a horrible death. Her demise will not haunt me however, because I, once again, marked her very location on a map, pointing you in her direction. Could you follow the simplest instructions needed to keep her alive until she was found? No. You had to elevate yourselves above the victim; place your own needs above hers. You sicken me; all of you, sicken me."

With leaden steps, Daniel left the apartment. It was time to change his identity again and then take the necessary steps to leave Atlanta for good. When he reached the parking lot, he decided to leave his car and head off on foot. He needed the walk to clear the anger and sorrow from his brain.

A quick look both ways and he bolted across Highland Avenue and briskly walked toward Highland Market. It wasn't a huge market, like Kroger or Piggly Wiggly, so he could only hope they'd have hair dye. Not all small marketplaces did. If not, he'd have to hop in his car to reach the nearest sizable grocery store. He was nearing the market when he spotted Salon Modello.

"I've never had my hair professionally tended before," he murmured. "Might be just the thing I need to lift my spirits a bit. If they take walk-ins."

He entered the salon and two men eagerly jumped up to greet him, neither of whom appeared busy at present.

"Can you squeeze in a last-minute appointment for a cut and dye? I'm feeling a bit down and I need a good pick-me-up," Daniel stated, pulling two one-hundred-dollar bills from his wallet.

"Absolutely, which of us would you prefer do the job?"

"One can wash and cut and the other color? Sound reasonable?"

Daniel held the bills out, one toward each man. They took the proffer and set about reinventing Daniel into yet another man that would be unrecognizable to anyone who'd come into prior contact with Christian Price or his real persona.

"Have you heard about what's happening at the police department?" Price queried as the one man massaged his scalp with shampoo. As long as he was working to relax his agitation, he may as well get a feel for how the public felt about the ineptitude of their guardians.

"Hell yeah," the stylist exclaimed. "That's one sick, twisted, son-of-a-bitch."

"Maybe, but what about the police? They're no better, letting those women die, and just before I came in here, I saw on the news that they'd turned the lights back on at the precinct. Sounds to me like they don't give a shit about their officer."

"Lean your head back a little," the stylist instructed, then set to rinsing the shampoo from Christian's hair. "Maybe the lights are back on," the stylist continued, pulling a towel from a shelf overhead, "because they've located the officer already. I mean, isn't that possible?

And they just haven't gotten around to flipping all the breakers again yet?"

Christian was shaken into silence. First, he hadn't expected anyone to defend the police; and second, he hadn't anticipated that they'd locate his latest victim so quickly. It didn't register that it would be possible. If that were the case, and the lights did signal a speedy end, they'd likely turn their focus toward finding him. He still needed a change of appearance to get out of town without being identified, so he'd stay and finish his makeover. Once done, he'd need to get his gear together and move on before the police threw a dragnet around the city and apprehended him.

When he headed back to the apartment an hour and a half later his spirits had lifted a bit at the knowledge that the police officer's son wouldn't be left without a mother; and he determined that to keep his spirits up, he would not view the television news again until he settled over the border in Tennessee. Not only was it a waste of his time, but he couldn't risk hearing that the search for him was now the primary focus.

He paid a visit to the bathroom to ensure his tenant was still sleeping, then slowly set about packing up his gear, following his normal routine for abandoning a property. After his equipment was stowed by the front door, he did a walk through, making certain that no sign of his existence remained, down to emptying all of the trash receptacles. His last stop, as always, was to ensure that his unwilling and unconscious host would remain asleep for at least several hours after his departure.

He took another syringe, filled the veins of the man still sleeping soundly, and then began to transport his belongings to his vehicle, peering carefully about each time he left the apartment.

When everything was cleared out, he punched in the shortest route to the Tennessee border into his GPS and then pulled out of the complex.

"Goodbye Atlanta. I do feel sorry for the residents that inhabit this thoroughly unprotected city." With a heavy sigh, he took the ramp for I-75 and headed north. It was time to start planning for his next experiment in a new city, "but this time, I need to formulate a method by which the police actually need to do some detecting."

CHAPTER 35

Hardwick sat down at the computer and waited for the electricity to come back on. When it did, he wasted no time turning on his computer.

"Where do you want us?" Harding asked, standing as soon as the lights came on.

"Just do what the captain suggested. Start a search of the building. Wilson, you and Cortez head outside to search the grounds first. He may not have been able to infiltrate the building, but there are sources of power outside that he could utilize."

"Sounds good," the captain concurred, coming into the bullpen. "Harding and I will start on the second floor and work our way down to the lower level. "Wilson and

Cortez can join us as soon as they're done outside. And Hardwick..."

"Yes, Captain?"

"I do hope this idea of yours bears fruit. We're a laughingstock among other precincts right now; our reputation in tatters. It wouldn't hurt to get this one right and apprehend the bad guy while we're at it."

"I'm with you, Captain."

"Good, then let's get to it."

Hardwick punched up the police database for the east coast and typed in his new search parameters. He kept the age range, because he was still convinced that the man in question was thirty to fifty years of age, and to within the past twenty years; but this time, he added his new information on the potential suspect. When done, he half expected the computer to find his request for unsolved homicides with a scientist's spouse as soon as he finished typing. When the computer came back with a negative result, Hardwick slammed his fists down on his desk; loud enough to echo through the halls of the empty department; also, to elicit cry outs from his captain and Harding from one floor up.

"Everything good down there, Hardwick?"

"Yeah, just peachy," Hardwick yelled back. He shook his head, drew in a deep breath, and then decided to try to access the central U.S. police database. "Just because he did his dirty work along the east coast, doesn't mean he hails from here," he murmured to himself, retyping all his search parameters.

This time, the computer spat out a single name. Hardwick was so stunned that he sat staring at the system for the longest time, nearly in shock. The face that popped up, however, bore no resemblance to the drawing given by the priest, which had Hardwick doubting his search yet again. Still, he had to be certain, so he tried to access the file.

The words *Access Denied* flashed before his eyes and he wanted to throw the monitor across the room, "I should have known that interstate access would be trickier than I wanted it to be. Captain!" He yelled loudly and immediately heard footsteps descending the staircase.

"What gives, Hardwick?" The captain asked; he and Harding weaving through the desks in the bullpen.

"I think I found our perp, but I don't have access to the file. I need you to call the Chicago PD and request a copy."

"You found him? Really?" Harding asked, plopping down in a chair across from Hardwick's desk.

"Yeah, if it's our guy, I guess he really is a scientist, or was. The information I was able to access is sparse. His name is Daniel Whittaker. Here's his picture." Hardwick turned the monitor so that Harding could see the face.

"That doesn't look anything like the sketch the priest gave us," Harding replied, looking at the photo on the screen carefully. "That man has dark brown hair and wire-rimmed glasses...I can't quite make out the color of his eyes. He's pasty though, which is how I imagine a scientist to be, but he doesn't look like a weakling. How tall is he?" Harding continued, scanning what little information was available. "Doesn't say here, but he looks like he could be about as tall as the priest said. The sketch the priest provided showed our perp had longish blonde hair and said nothing about glasses. Contacts maybe... shit...are we sure this is our guy?"

"Not right now, but that means that either two scientists were involved in an unsolved murder, the priest got it wrong; or this isn't our perp."

"Well, I'll requisition the file from the Chicago PD. Hopefully there won't be any hoop jumping involved." The captain headed for his office, "Oh, while I'm making the call, you two can resume searching the building."

"Think we should search this floor?" Harding asked, as they stood to head toward the stairwell. "I mean, it's mostly open area. Surely, we'd have spotted someone tied to an electrical device if they were around here, right?"

"Did you and the captain finish upstairs?" Hardwick asked.

"Yeah, no nooks or crannies that a person could stuff another person where they'd go unnoticed. I think that Wilson is right. There's no way that Price could've gotten a person in here and set up an elaborate death set-up without being spotted."

Hardwick stopped walking, "He would've had to do so without being spotted—or noticed."

"Now what are you thinking?"

"It's simple enough to determine whether there was a breach here at the station by examining security footage from the day of the abduction."

"We don't know when our officer was abducted, only when we were told to start searching for him or her," Harding interjected, and Hardwick let out a string of curses.

"Okay," Hardwick backtracked after calming himself down, "we start by reviewing footage from yesterday and today. If we find nothing suspicious, we go back a day further. I don't think it likely he could hold onto one of our officers for too long without someone noticing."

"Where do they keep the recorder?" Harding asked.

"Security. Top floor. I say we head up and review the day's footage first. It may not be a complete time-saver, but it's better than doing a blind search of a building this size," Hardwick said, hitting the up arrow on the elevator.

"Like the rest of the squad is doing? And why aren't we taking the stairs? You getting too decrepit to climb stairs now, old man?"

"Strained my knee playing handball," Hardwick explained, stepping into the elevator car. "You're welcome to hike up if you want to?"

Harding laughed and jumped into the car as the doors were sliding closed. They reached the upper level quickly and immediately set to viewing the security footage

They were part way through the footage when the captain joined them, followed by Wilson and Cortez.

"How'd you know we were up here?" Harding asked.

"You weren't in the bullpen," the captain explained.

"You already searched every level?" Hardwick asked.

"Just a cursory look," the captain admitted. "When we didn't spot y'all down there, we figured you must have had another idea that proved a distraction, so did you find anything of value?"

"I may have, yeah," Hardwick said thoughtfully. He rewound the footage to 4:35 p.m. "Watch here." He pointed to the front lobby and then traced his finger along with a man carrying a toolbox.

"Maintenance? What's weird about that?" Wilson asked.

"Nothing yet, but look now," he said, fast forwarding to time stamp 7:15 p.m. "The maintenance man returns..."

"I'm not following the significance either," Cortez interjected.

"Just watch," Hardwick stated. "He appears to engage in banter with Sergeant Stevens and then...here...look. He meets up with one of our *female* officers, who appears to be waiting for him by the stairwell."

"Shit," Wilson exclaims softly.

"Yeah," Hardwick concurs. "Now watch," he says, fast forwarding to just after the lights go out. "It's hard to see, but it appears that the maintenance man returns from downstairs—alone."

"It may be significant in that it raises the probability of someone getting inside, but it does little in providing an identity, or proving that Price placed the latest victim within our precinct," the captain murmured.

"I didn't know our cameras were on a separate power supply," Harding noted off-handed.

"Yeah," the captain said, "We thought it best in the event of a power outage."

"It's a good thing too, or we'd have never known

about this. I say we head down to lower storage level. See if it bears fruit?"

"It better," the captain added, "because I just got a radio update from the officers in the field. They're nearly halfway through the search and no sign of our missing officer."

"What's the word from Chicago?" Hardwick asked as they filed out of the security office.

"What about Chicago?" Wilson queried.

"I followed up on that hunch I had and got a hit. It led to an open case in Chicago."

"Well, I'll be damned," Wilson muttered.

"I gave the sergeant there the case file number. He said he'd be in touch soon," the captain replied.

Hardwick hit the down elevator button and Harding laughed, "He's too old to take the stairs."

"Laugh it up, Chuckles," Hardwick quipped.

"Well, it *was* installed for the handicapped," Cortez laughed.

"Yeah, well since you two are in such tip-top shape, why don't you run on down the stairs, and I'll meet up with you," Hardwick said, preparing the enter the car.

"Sorry, Hardwick," the captain interrupted, "bum knee or no, you're going to have to take the stairs with us."

Hardwick didn't respond and eyed the captain quizzically.

The captain sighed, "I still think it highly unlikely that Price was the maintenance man, or that he managed to stash his victim here in the precinct; however, with that being said, the probability of him doing so is greater now in my opinion than it was an hour ago. And since the elevator runs on electricity, we can't take the chance."

Hardwick nodded, "Understood."

"Well, let's head down to see what we find. Last one down is a rotten egg," Harding quipped.

"Wow, really?" Cortez replied, shaking his head. "I thought you had to be out of puberty to work for the Atlanta PD."

"Come on, y'all, let's show a little respect for the investigation," the captain snapped, shaking his head in bemusement; however, none of the detectives, nor the captain, genuinely believed that they would find anything in the precinct.

CHAPTER 36

J ust shy of two hours after leaving Atlanta, Price crossed over the border into Tennessee and immediately began considering where he'd stop and hole up for the night. He normally avoided motels after he started his abductions, because he worried that motels would be on the list of high-priority searches when attempting to locate a perpetrator; especially when it was known that the perp was from out of town. That's why he always borrowed an apartment while he did his work. When he first arrived in a new city, however, he didn't have to worry about local law enforcement discovering him and took advantage of more comfortable accommodations. He grinned when he spotted a

Cracker Barrel near the motel and decided he'd eat breakfast there the following morning.

"First things first though, I need to check in and then see where the investigation in Atlanta stands."

"Help you, sir?" The concierge greeted.

"I need a room for one night. Non-smoking. Do you have a king-sized bed available?"

"One moment and I'll check for you." The young man started punching at his keyboard. After a few minutes, he looked up with a smile, "I do have a King-sized bed available, yes. If you will fill in this form, I'll be happy to get you registered. If I could just get your credit card, please?"

"I'll pay with cash," Daniel replied instinctively.

"Very good, sir, but I'll still need a card on file. We won't, of course, make any charges..."

"Unless I damage the room or rent porn videos, yes, I know," Daniel interjected, pulling out his Visa. He slid it across the desk and then picked up the pen and started filling out the form. After what seemed an interminable amount of time, the concierge concluded the computer entries and then slid over an electronic key. "You'll be in room 117," he stated politely. "Enjoy your stay."

Daniel picked up the flat piece of plastic and then departed, pulling his car in front of his assigned room. Without bothering to collect his bags, he went inside and immediately turned on the television. His channel search was a little frantic, because it didn't register on his departure from Georgia, that he might not be able to pick up the Atlanta's WAGA news channel.

He flipped channels for a while but did not find any news broadcasts in progress. A glance at his watch revealed why—it was just after 10:30 p.m. It was past time for some broadcasts, and too early for anything coming out of Atlanta. He tossed the remote on the bed with a sigh and then went to retrieve his baggage. The next half hour was going to be the hardest of his life, waiting to learn the fate of Lucia, and he prayed fervently that she had indeed been located.

CHAPTER 37

A nything?" The captain called from behind an old desk chair.

Harding popped up from behind a filing cabinet, "Nothing over here."

"Someone hand me a flashlight. I left mine upstairs," Hardwick called. "There's a closet over here, but the bulb is missing."

"Figures we'd walk right by a closet; the logical place to hide someone," Cortez griped, handing Hardwick his flashlight.

"Yeah, but you're presupposing that there is someone to find," Harding replied. "The recording may have been just..."

Everyone, get over here!" Hardwick exclaimed the

moment the light infiltrated the small room. "Looks like someone cut through the sheetrock. Could be nothing, but I need something to pull it back."

"You've got to be freakin' kidding me," Harding exclaimed as Wilson pushed past him.

"I have a switchblade," he said, reaching into the room. "That do?"

"Yes," Hardwick said, snatching the blade and handing the flashlight over, "Aim this over here."

Hardwick stuck the switchblade along the seam in the sheetrock and tugged, breaking off a section. He closed his eyes and sighed in frustration. He closed the switchblade and tossed it on the ground and then slid his fingers into the opening he'd created, pulling the sheetrock open.

Every man let out a string of curses at seeing the figure strapped to the buffer.

"Shit, shit, shit, I can't believe I almost took the elevator down. The impact would have pulverized her head. Shit."

"If anyone is culpable here," the captain interjected, "it's me. I'm the one who naïvely believed Price wasn't capable of this level of infiltration; that he couldn't pull this off. Not here. Not beneath our noses. And because of my naïve assumption, I arrogantly presumed I could ignore the warnings to leave the electricity off. My ignorance nearly got my officer killed. I'm no better than the two officers I fired."

"Sir, she isn't dead. We got to her in time," Cortez offered in sympathy. "That's what we should focus on. And you stopped Hardwick from squishing her like a bug, remember?"

Hardwick picked the switchblade back up, slipped inside the opening, and then set about carefully cutting through the layers of duct tape. When he'd freed her body and head, he carefully lowered her to the ground. He wasn't worried about the remainder of the tape, rather with getting out of that area.

"Someone lean in and grab...Officer Mendocino," Hardwick continued after reading her name plate, "beneath the arms and pull her through. Be careful of the loose duct tape surrounding her head; don't let it get hung up on anything."

Wilson leaned in and grabbed hold of the officer. "Someone might consider calling an ambulance," he called behind him, "she's pretty out of it."

"On it," Cortez replied, racing upstairs.

As soon as Mendocino was clear, Wilson dragged her out of the closet, laying her on the corridor floor. He immediately did a check of her vitals, "She's breathing steady; just unconscious. If someone will grab a pair of scissors, I'll start cutting away this duct tape," he offered.

"Use the switchblade," Harding offered.

"Might be safer to use scissors. I'm going to have to cut off a lot of her hair and if I have to get close to her scalp..."

"I'll grab a pair," Harding offered and ran off.

While he waited, Wilson started working to remove the tape surrounding her abdomen, "Now that we have a potential suspect, we should move heaven and earth to find that son-of-a-bitch before he has a chance to strike at us again."

Hardwick collapsed against the wall; his relief nearly more than he could take. "We should get forensics down here," he muttered after a few minutes. "I looked around a bit. There's an IV drip in there that needs analyzing. You said she was ok?"

Wilson nodded, "Just a bit sticky," he added, pulling the remainder of the tape away, just as Harding returned.

"We should also call in all officers now, so that we can shift our focus to finding Price," Harding said, his hostility towards the perp thick.

Hardwick shook his head, "No, he's gone. He probably fled as soon as the power went out."

"What makes you assume that, especially when we were wrong about this?" The captain asked sharply.

"He didn't just spoon-feed us clues this time, he all but handed our officer to us on a silver platter. He contained the search area to within reasonable bounds and by instructing us to keep the power off until the search was concluded, he ensured her safety; knowing that we'd not likely endanger one of our own."

"But we did," the captain muttered.

"Yeah, we did," Hardwick sighed, "but fortunately she wasn't harmed by our arrogance or our stupidity; and he wouldn't know that."

"So then, what do we do now?" Wilson asked, carefully trimming the tape from Mendocino's hair. She may not have intended it, but she was going to have a pixie cut by the time he was through.

"We thank our lucky stars that he's gone from our district, and then we flood every police outlet with an all-points bulletin, identifying our prime suspect."

The captain nodded, "Okay, I'll get that done as soon as the paramedics take care of Officer Mendocino."

"They're en route. Five minutes out," Cortez said, his breathing heavy from racing up and down the stairs.

"Cortez, you and Harding can go and inform her family of what's transpired, and escort them to Piedmont hospital. Then all of you go home and get some rest. Come tomorrow morning, gentlemen, we begin an overhaul of our precinct. I want brainstorming that will cause thunderstorms in the area. We will go over every infinitesimal detail of every search we conducted and will generate a plan to improve upon our performance. We will train and re-train, until we are better than a well-oiled machine. This will never happen on my watch again."

"Do you think we'll hear from Price again?" Cortez asked.

Hardwick nodded, "He can't wash his hands of us entirely until he knows Officer Mendocino's fate. He'll call. I'm tempted to see if he'll do something rash if I tell him we failed."

"Like what? Turn himself in?" Wilson replied sarcastically, snipping, and tossing aside the remainder of the tape. He sat back on his haunches and sighed loudly.

No one responded to Wilson's sarcasm, merely sat staring at the officer lying on the floor, her hair in taped clumps nearby. It took a few minutes before the shock wore off.

"Captain," Hardwick said softly, "I know you want us to head home, but I think I'll stay to finish some paperwork. Something tells me that we haven't heard the last from this guy."

"Yeah," Cortez added. "Mind if we send a couple of uniforms to inform the Mendocino family? I'd like to stay too."

"Yeah, me too," Harding added.

The captain eyed his officers for a moment and then

nodded. "We'll see this finished—hopefully—and then get some rest."

The men stood to follow the paramedics, who'd arrived and, after a quick assessment, loaded Mendocino onto a stretcher and headed up the stairs. Hardwick nearly punched the up button on the elevator, instinctively favoring his aching knee, but after nearly killing a fellow officer; he wasn't certain when he'd be able to use an elevator again—anytime soon. A glance at the faces of his fellow detectives revealed they were of the same mind. They all walked up the stairs, the events of the last two weeks weighing heavily on their hearts and minds.

CHAPTER 38

D aniel was beside himself with questions. He'd flipped on the television at precisely 11 p.m., but he hadn't been able to locate the Atlanta news network. In fact, he'd only been able to pick up about four local channels because, in his haste, he'd chosen a motel with no cable. He was livid. He reached for his disposable cell, but then realized that he'd done what he always did—disposed of his disposable cell before departing a city in which he'd concluded testing.

He picked up the receiver from the phone on the nightstand and dialed the front desk. When the night manager answered, he immediately launched into a tirade, "Clearly displayed on your sign out front are the words "Cable TV", yet here I sit in my room with absolutely no cable television."

My apologies sir, the concierge replied politely, *but our cable is out. We had a storm blow through earlier today that knocked out service to most of the area.*

"And you didn't bother to inform me when I checked in? Next, you'll be telling me that the storm washed away your food stores and you won't be offering a free breakfast either."

My apologies again, sir. If it'll assist any, I'll be happy to take twenty... Before the clerk could conclude his offer, Daniel hung up. He gathered up his wallet and jacket and then headed out. He was so agitated at being in the dark, that he nearly forgot that he was in a foreign city, and it was rapidly approaching midnight. He nearly returned to his room, but a glance down the backstreet where his motel was nestled revealed the lights of a convenience store on the other side of the main road, so instead of heading back to his room, he headed for his car instead. He wasn't a drinker, but not knowing what was happening in Atlanta made him want to purchase a six-pack and drink every single can within minutes.

He pulled into the deserted parking lot and headed inside the equally deserted store.

"Evening," the woman behind the register muttered unenthusiastically. "Help you?"

"Can you exchange this for a roll of quarters please?" Daniel requested politely, placing a ten-dollar bill on the counter, "and point me toward a pay phone?"

"I ain't supposed to give out our quarters," she said in a tone that suggested that even a moron knew that.

He closed his eyes and drew in a deep breath, "I need to make an urgent long distance phone call, or I wouldn't bother you for the quarters." He slid another ten from his wallet and placed it next to the other. "For you; for your trouble."

She picked up the one bill and slid it into her pocket, and then went to the register to exchange it for the quarters: muttering beneath her breath about people buying cell phones nowadays for a reason. She placed the quarters on the counter, and then returned to her chair, completely disinterested in assisting him further.

"The pay phone?"

"Ain't got one here. The nearest one I know of is down the road a spell. Down at the Cracker Barrel."

Daniel picked up the quarters and slid them into his pocket.

"Do you have a location around here that sells burner phones? Pay-as-you-go type deals?"

"Nothing open at this hour," the clerk replied, and Daniel thought of the adage of pulling teeth.

"I was thinking more along the lines of when things did open," he said, trying to keep his manner polite.

The clerk sighed, annoyed at being bothered. It was apparent by her apathy that she chose this shift because she wasn't a people person, "there's a Walmart down the road from the Cracker Barrel. They might have something."

"Thanks," Christian replied and headed toward the exit. When he reached the door, he turned back and cleared his throat loudly. When she looked up, he pointed left and then right, "Cracker Barrel?"

She returned the gesture by pointing left "...down Ringgold."

"Thanks," he muttered, and headed for the car.

Less than ten minutes later, he spotted the Cracker Barrel's empty parking lot and pulled in. He slowly drove the length of the building, and finally spotted the phone booth near the front entrance.

He pulled over, turned off his car, and slid out. He dug in his pants pocket and pulled out the paper upon which he'd written the Atlanta Police Department's phone number, something he nearly forgot to do before he disposed of his disposable phone. There certainly weren't enough coins in his pocket to dial directory assistance first. He laid the paper on the tiny ledge while he unrolled his coins. He fed the coins into the slot; then set about dialing the number.

Atlanta Police Department, Zone 5.

"This is Christian Price..."

Hold please.

While he waited, he tapped the ledge in impatience. He'd not used a payphone in more than a decade, but he knew that the calls weren't cheap, and he didn't want this call interrupted. A minute later, the transferred call was answered.

Detective Hardwick

"Well, Detective, still at your desk after midnight? I'm not certain whether that translates to good news or bad. Still, you can guess why I'm calling?"

To confess your crimes and turn yourself in?

"Touché, Detective, but no; I am merely calling to inquire as to the well-being of Office Mendocino. I assume that the search was successful, especially as I saw, before departing Atlanta, that the lights in your precinct shone brightly?" There was an accusatory tone in Price's query that Hardwick didn't overlook.

I figured a man like you would be all over the news and would know immediately whether we'd located her.

"You've located her alive, I trust?"

Do you really care?

"I get that you're attempting to stall, Detective; to

attempt to run a trace on my location, so I'll be candid. Even if you managed to run a trace, I already stated that I'm no longer within reach of the Atlanta Police Department and am going to be long gone from this place also, very soon; so, you may as well let me know whether you found your officer alive, since it isn't a likelihood that you'll be able to find me. I must confess to being furious at seeing those lights blazing. Quite disheartening. I also must confess to being outraged at knowing you blatantly ignored my instructions for a complete power outage.

So, if you weren't certain as to the outcome of the search, why did you leave Atlanta? I thought you didn't quit if the police department continued to fail in its efforts.

Daniel sighed heavily, "Sadly, I felt as if your department was beyond hope."

Hardwick's mind immediately agreed, which caused him to shake himself mentally in anger. He'd never failed so miserably at any investigation and that had him questioning his own competence, which made him feel worthless. He certainly didn't need a murderer confirming those feelings.

Your opinion is worth squat, he spat in reply.

"Maybe, but I'll disagree. You know, I tried desperately to set you on a path to betterment, but my efforts were a complete failure. Thus, I felt it prudent to move on. Now, I'm going to hang up in just a moment, but I would like to know whether your officer is alive.

I just bet you would. Well, you know what? You'll have to find your information from a different news source. I'm not interested in easing your conscious—Daniel.

The line went dead, and Daniel stood for a moment staring slack-jawed at the receiver in his hand. After a moment, he grinned, but it lacked any humor, "Kudos, Detective. No one prior has ascertained my identity. Well done." He replaced the receiver, but his anger quickly elevated again at not having received the answers he sought. He would, indeed, need to locate an alternate source for his answers, but it wouldn't come from the place he was staying the night, with no cable. Perhaps the Wi-Fi would be up, and he could locate a web-broadcast of the Atlanta news. If not, he'd need to find different motel in a different city, tonight, and set the alarm for early tomorrow morning. He couldn't go too far, or he'd be outside the Atlanta viewing area. He wouldn't sleep anyway until he knew.

"Gives me your money," an African American man in tattered clothing spat at him from between two missing front teeth.

"How about I just give you some money for booze?" Daniel patronized, pulling out his wallet. He was angry and in no mood to pander to the needs of the local degenerates. Had anger not overshadowed his common sense, he'd have thought twice about enraging a homeless man.

"What? Yous think that just 'cause I's in a hard way that I be a drunk or sumpin? Whos you think you is anyways?"

"Fine, you don't need money for booze. I'll just give you a twenty for whatever it is you need money for." Daniel sifted through the bills in his wallet, searching for the smaller denominations. He tossed the money at the man and then started toward his car. The man stepped in front of him.

"And I says to give me the whole damned thing," the man snapped, snatching at the wallet in Daniel's hand.

Daniel's reflexes were sharp, and he jerked back, "And I say that if you're going to demand a hand-out, the least you can do is take what you're offered."

"You thinkin' that just because we homeless that we ain't got our pride?" Another voice interjected, slamming a foot into Daniel's back. "You think that you can just throw money at us like we're nothing?"

Daniel hadn't realized that there were two homeless men, which had likely been the intent. Keep him preoccupied so that the other could render him defenseless. It worked. Daniel had been completely unprepared for the ambush from behind. He fell to his knees as the throbbing in his back shot up his spine.

The man in front brought his knee up and rammed it into his face, breaking his nose. Daniel fell on his back, his vision blurring from the pain somersaulting through his head.

The second man slammed his foot into Daniel's side, and he bent over, and then another blow landed, and another. Daniel curled in on himself, trying to protect his body from the pounding of flailing feet, but his efforts were ineffectual. He felt ribs crack and bones snap and wondered how battered he'd have to be before the two assailants stopped their abuse. Then they did stop.

"Shoulda just given me the damned money," the first homeless man snarled, without remorse, then reached down and snatched the wallet from the ground. The man turned away and Daniel was grateful it was over and that he would live, until the second man bent down next to him, eyeing him coldly.

The dirty-faced white kid cocked his head side-to-side, without uttering a word, watching Daniel intently. Then he grinned and reached behind his back and slowly retracted a long blade from his pant pocket. He held it beneath Daniel's nose, twisting it back and forth, flicking the tip threateningly beneath his nostrils.

"Let's go!" The older African American called, pulling the cash from the billfold. He flicked the empty wallet at Daniel's beaten body.

"He's a witness!" The kid called back.

Daniel stared at the boy, who couldn't have been more than seventeen. He wanted to say something— barter for his life, but they'd already taken his wallet, so he had nothing left with which to barter. As if the kid read his thoughts, he grinned again, and jammed the knife into the side of his throat, then just as quickly, pulled it free and stepped back, watching the arterial spurt with a macabre fascination.

Son-of-a-bitch. Daniel mentally screamed. He threw his hand over the wound, trying to stop his life's blood spurting from his body. Tears glistened in his eyes as his vision started to blur. *Son-of-a-bitch! Now I'll never know if she lived.*

CHAPTER 39

Detectives! In here now!" The captain called loudly from his office. He was in the process of turning up the volume when his detectives sprinted in.

That's right, Patricia. This is quite a surprise for everyone here at Channel 5 who knew the perpetrator as Christian Price; and were it not for an anonymous tip that came into the newsroom incredibly early this morning, we never would have made the connection.

"What's going on?" Wilson asked.

"Shh, listen." The captain said, his gaze pinned to the television.

Again, for those of you just joining us, we've received reports from our sister station in Chattanooga, Tennessee that police in the small suburb of East Ridge found the body of

Daniel Whittaker shortly before 1 a.m.; the serial killer that we, in Atlanta, knew by the moniker Christian Price. Police say that Whittaker was the victim of a mugging and was stabbed to death outside a local Cracker Barrel supermarket off Ringgold Road.

We, at Channel 5, were astonished to learn that Daniel Whittaker was a scientist from Chicago who went missing shortly after the death of his wife, who was murdered. Her case remains unsolved. We have also learned that, in his role of scientist, Whittaker often worked with the U.S. military on developing methods in which to perfect torture techniques to obtain information from terrorists. The media in his home state of Illinois often criticized him regarding the use of human subjects in his experiments. Whittaker was forty-seven years old.

The captain reached over and retrieved the remote, turning off the television before facing his detectives.

"I'm trying not to get up and dance a jig," he grinned.

"Karma's a bitch," Harding said in a self-satisfied tone.

"I take it you leaked the identity to the media?" Wilson asked, addressing Hardwick.

Hardwick nodded, "Figures you'd jump to the assumption that I did that."

"Call it a hunch," Wilson replied, "but I have a feeling

that you weren't going to let this guy get free of our clutches without a fight."

Hardwick grinned, "I couldn't let it go, no. I needed the citizens of Atlanta to know they were safe now; and the best way to do that was to let them know that Christian Price was dead."

"Even though we hadn't gotten the report from Chicago PD yet as to whether Whittaker was indeed our perp?"

Hardwick nodded again, "Maybe I was risking something by playing that gut feeling, but when I typed in the search parameters and only one name came up, I'd say it was a fair intuition."

"What if you're wrong? What if Whittaker wasn't Price?" Wilson prodded. "What if the guy in Chicago was simply a man who lost his wife and has nothing to do with this case whatsoever?"

"You never let things go, do you?" Cortez snapped. "Give the man a little credit, will you? He wouldn't have leaked it if his intuition weren't backed up by something solid."

"Indeed," Hardwick said with a satisfied grin.

"How can you be so damned certain?" Wilson snapped.

"Price...Whittaker...had an inclination that I started a trace on his location the minute he called. Since he was calling from a phone booth, so he was convinced the trace wouldn't bear fruit. He all but told me that I could run a trace because he wasn't in our jurisdiction any longer. Just before I disconnected the call, the trace came back as a payphone in East Ridge, Tennessee."

"There could be hundreds of phone booths in..." Wilson started.

"East Ridge," Hardwick interrupted, "is a small city, with only about 21,000 residents and a whopping eleven phone booths. Most located along the stretch where Whittaker happened to be calling from—Ringgold Road. So, do you think it would be difficult for police to run down eleven phone booths rather quickly, given the proper impetus?"

"What impetus would that be?" The captain chimed in.

"Once the trace pinpointed a general location, I immediately placed a call to their local police department and told them to be on the lookout for him. Told them what he'd done here, which must have spurred them into finding him fast because I'm certain they didn't want him setting up shop in their town. Anyway, they must have made a swing by the Cracker Barrel first thing after I called and found a body..."

"Okay, so a guy got mugged and killed," Wilson persisted in his usual antagonistic fashion, "that doesn't automatically make him our perp, especially since we don't know what our perp looks like—precisely. Too many different descriptions. And he could have changed his appearance again shortly after leaving Atlanta."

Hardwick grinned wide, refusing to allow Wilson to bait him. It was the first sincere smile he'd had since the whole affair with Price started, "It's Price, and Price is Whittaker, and Whittaker is our serial killer. Why? Because first, our serial killer called from one of their eleven phone booths. Not too many people were making calls after midnight in East Ridge, Tennessee. Second, this guy gets killed right next to a phone booth; and third, the police called and told me it was Whittaker just before I leaked the news story here to Channel 5."

"They couldn't have run his fingerprints..."

"Didn't have to," Hardwick interjected. "He was using his own car; registered in his own name."

"Arrogant son-of-a-bitch," Harding said, shaking his head.

"You could've easily been wrong," Wilson reprimanded, refusing to let the matter end.

"Yeah, well he wasn't wrong, so just drop it, Wilson," Harding defended.

"Hey, did you arrange the mugging too?" Cortez quipped, satisfied that they'd gotten their man.

"If only I'd thought of it. It would have been poetic justice, in my humble opinion," Hardwick said sincerely.

"It still was poetic," the captain interjected, "in my not-so humble opinion. Price...or Whittaker...whoever he was, met a justifiable end. He spent years murdering innocents in the name of perverted justice. He got what was coming to him."

"Yeah, like I said, Karma's a bitch," Harding repeated.

"You four, go home now," the captain said. "Take the day off. The case is finally over. When you come in tomorrow, I expect to hear some really good ideas on how to make this department..."

"...a well-oiled machine," Hardwick finished.

The captain nodded.

"Yes, Captain." Hardwick stood aside and shooed his fellow detectives from the captain's office.

"I don't know what he's talking about," Cortez whined, good-naturedly, as he passed, "I *am* a well-oiled machine."

Hardwick trailed behind, grinning sadly. Today he'd enjoy the banter and the relief at knowing another serial killer was put out of commission; but his sadness stemmed from knowing that he wasn't the man that meted justice. He was also contending with the reality that he'd made some grave errors in judgment; errors he'd never made before; errors that had him questioning whether it was time to retire.

Tomorrow the captain wanted changes, and he planned to give him a major one.

Tomorrow, he planned to resign.

ABOUT THE AUTHOR

Barbara Woster is an author as well as an educator and business owner. Writing is her passion and she's been doing this since she was 21 years old when she dreamed, and then penned, her first novel, *Dreamer of Destiny.*

Barbara also loves to read many different types of books, which carries over to her writing, so she doesn't just write in one genre rather preferring to write as ideas come to her, whether this turns out to be a romance, crime thriller, or middle grade work. She does, however, prefer suspense, so while many of her books may hold an element of romance, that tends to be a smaller piece of the overall story.

To find more titles by this author, visit her website @ https://barbarawosterauthor.com.

Lightning Source UK Ltd.
Milton Keynes UK
UKHW011837090223
416719UK00001B/207